STEVEN DE.

SUBMIT
HORROR

- THE 4TH COLLECTION -

CONTENTS

SHOOTING THE P.I.

The polystyrene cup of coffee left a ringed residue upon the car's dashboard under the hanging dice. Sipping the hot beverage, John caught sight of the two single pips on the foam ornaments dangling from the rear-view mirror: *Snake eyes; roll again*, he mused, licking his warmed lips.

Night-time had slipped over without warning, it seemed. John had spent most of that evening concentrating on the top windows of the second last house on Clive Street to have noticed the shift in daylight. But more important than the clock was for John Dunn, private investigator to the layman, to *clinically* stake out the location of his new client's wife on certain nights. The client had called him one morning not-so-long-ago to procure the P.I.'s services so that he could find out where his darling wife was of evenings–and with whom.

He caught sight of his subject once or twice: a silhouette of lovers embracing; her long. flowing hair; her lover's half crown. They shifted from room to room, unaware that their movements were being watched, even *recorded...* They moved with ease out of their hot and heavy lovemaking. John noted everything by pen and with photographs.

His client would be pleased, or contrarily displeased, whichever way you looked at it. On one hand, John had secured what had been paid for: definitive proof of adultery by a man who paid upfront and in cash. But on the other, John suspected that this raft of newfound information would break his client's heart and, without doubt, his trust in marriage, perhaps leading to the divorce courts without so much as a second thought.

The light from the upper window of the second last house on Clive Street went out before 1am. It appeared that the lovers had finished for sleep; the house remained still and was plunged into a somnolent darkness.

John's car startled the silence when he turned the key in the ignition. Yet unperturbed, he drove out of the street and into the mouth of the night.

The drive to his office the next morning was hampered by an intense sunshine that John countered with a low visor and cheap sunglasses. It was just too damn bright, too damn early.

John's office had been crafted in a space not nearly big enough–it was filled with more junk than anywhere that stored both use*ful* and use*less* shit. But it suited him. The lease was forgiving, the utilities mostly unused; and it was central, meaning he was easily accessible to anyone and everyone with genuine missing persons cases or just simple benefit fraud work. None of his business was ever tasking, especially when he trusted in his Nikon D3300, that could snap secrets in a flash.

Sometime after 10am, the phone rang. John picked up the receiver. The voice on the other end was forward and familiar. When the conversation ended, John hung up first, perplexed; exhausted. The stake-out the night before had been a 'success', but it normally resulted in the sacrifice of a good night's sleep and lack of energy the following morning. And he was losing weight. Not much–just a few millimetres' more when tightening his belt each morning.

John eventually decided on a mid-morning breakfast. He locked up the office and headed over to the diner across the road. He pushed open the glass-panelled door, which bumped and chimed the bell angled above it; there was a gathering of old sorts seated on the left, mingling and sipping their way through the 'buy one, get one free' coffee deal, munching with dentures on a cream bun or scone. John didn't feel like anything sweet this morning. In fact, even considering his weight loss, he didn't feel like piling on anything other than a bacon roll, and that was him *hungry*.

"Good morning, John," called the waitress, idling by the counter.

It wasn't the shop-standard apron colours that caught John's eye (it never was)–it was the waitress's copper red hair. Though health and safety rules permitted it from being free, he could see its radiance beneath the hairnet as bright as ever, coiled under the hairnet like a rat snake.

"Morning, Jess," he returned with a smile. There was no queue this morning to hide behind so his shyness would be exposed today. Of course, he couldn't tell exactly how flushed his cheeks were, but he could imagine he was stood there beaming like a beacon.

"What can I get you?" Jess asked, flipping open her notebook. She leaned against the counter, patient with her pen.

There was a menu laying before her (more under, as the booklet was trapped beneath her aproned chest and the glass-top counter); John reached forward to collect it, inhibited by the awkwardness that stalks such moments.

There wasn't much on the menu that took his fancy.

"Just a tea for now, please, Jess. No sugar; just milk."

She flashed him a smile.

"You sweet enough?"

He blushed again. He summoned the courage to wink at her, which probably came across inexperienced and a bit creepy. He took a seat beside the booth by the window and waited.

Jess brought his order over. She placed the cup and teapot down before playfully tugging his chin–the kind of pinch-grip an exotic dancer might lead with before she's teasing you into slipping fresh-drawn banknotes into her underwear.

"Had a bad night?" Jess asked, concern across her face.

"Is it *that* obvious?" John replied, warming his hands around the cup. "Yeah, I spent half the night awake. Didn't crash 'til probably around three this morning."

She exhibited a fleeting look of worry.

"I think you need to see the doctor, hon. Your eyes are carrying big bags underneath 'em. Won't be good for the complexion. Summer's almost here."

"I'll make an appointment as soon as I can," he told her, though he expected her to doubt him–he would, too.

John felt like just another lowly customer and likely not high on the waitress's people-and-things-to-see-and-do list. He was accustomed to knockbacks; oh, boy, he was; *So, Jess,* he thought, *just smile again, say* "I hope you do, John," *and be on your way.*

About five minutes later, the chimes above the door sounded. John took no notice at first until he saw the legs walk into view from behind the first booth. Smooth, black tights bathed them from their heels right up and under the hem of the pricey pencil skirt, where they either halted on each pin's thigh as tantalising hold ups or continued, firmly cinching the lady's waist–*her* waist; this elegant woman.

John had seen his new client's wife in person only once (the rest having been from photographs that had been passed to him, or from his own late-night detection 'collection'). So, he knew from looking at the woman in the diner now, it was the same woman who had shook his hand quite charily in the supermarket car park back then, who then hid from her husband a glare that made John suspect she knew just what her spouse was up to. *Because* she *was so innocent…*

The longer he held his breath, the slower it seemed for her to fully come into view. She seemed every bit 'high maintenance'. John inhaled massively–but not too obviously–when she stood in the centre of the diner. His eyes trailed the lurex back-seam along her calves that only made him wish that he were the lucky one with her hand in marriage.

Jess, the red-haired waitress looked over in John's direction. Had she seen him drooling over this fox in a pencil skirt? No… it looked as if she was directing the woman to John's table. *This is it!* he screamed inside. *I've been rumbled! I was instructed to deny everything*, he reminded himself. *Yes, that's it: deny everything.*

Her perfume fragrance–a uniting of jasmine and sandalwood, among other scents–met his nostrils before any eye contact was anticipated, for those eyes were now shielded by her black, slanted saucer-shaped hat. Its stylish, crin trim design said money. John knew each marital partner had an abundance of it.

She sat down opposite him in the booth unaware, as if she didn't want to or somehow couldn't, acknowledge John's presence. She was struggling whilst finding comfort with the faux leather seating.

"How did you find us?" she said in a low voice, keeping half her face hidden, remaining all mysterious and alluring.

Harbouring a stomach-shredding sensation, John watched as she removed her gloves. They slipped off with ease, revealing the smoothest tanned arms this side of a summer swimwear catalogue.

"Um, me?" he asked, quietly, like her.

She folded the gloves over, placing them neatly at the outer edge of the table.

"Look, I don't think it's fair that someone's spying on me again," she began. "You have no right! I have a life, too. Whether or not it's immoral, it's my life, and I make the decisions."

John felt shitty. Sure, it was his job and where he could utilise stealth and discretion in place of straight-up harassment and intimidation–not to mention concealment–each job usually ended with a high success rate for him.

"I don't know what you're talking about." *Yeah, John, keep tight-lipped, don't let anything slip.*

Jess came over to their table carrying the woman's cup and saucer on a tray. It seemed very O.T.T. for a rural café. The teapot, milk jug and sugar packets escorted the china on the tray.

The woman issued a polite acknowledgement and set about preparing her drink once the waitress had gone. John watched with fascination; he knew it was within his interests to get the hell out of there but sitting in the company of this pretty fox–just the two of them–set his heart fluttering and got his juices flowing.

She finished making her drink. She spoke, and again, quietly.

"Don't keep this up; it would be stupid of either of us to assume it will get any better…" She took a sip from her cup. "But it sure can get a lot worse."

"I still don't know what you're talking about."

"No? Are you sure?"

They had yet to make eye contact. Maybe she was embarrassed, humiliated, that her husband had somehow caught her? She was still a little shame-faced this morning, perhaps.

"If you'll excuse me, Miss," John said, shuffling along the seat on his way out of the booth.

"So, that's to be it?" said the woman, and this time she had sunk all the tea. There was not a drop left in the cup.

John kept silent, cool, and stood, attempting to make that desired eye-contact, even fleetingly. He felt that if he could share that with her, perhaps they could pursue a different line of questioning–maybe even elsewhere? What colour were they that day they had been introduced by her husband? Green? Like sparkling emeralds. Beautiful, green jewels.

Before John left the table, he brushed by her, and at that moment she whispered within earshot a message that carried with it a grim gravity:

"I'll kill you."

***

The diner trip had left John shook up and with more questions than answers, and he had an idea just where he could put some of those questions to bed.

Back in his office, he retrieved the phone number of his new client. Since the wife was likely still out of the house, he figured he could talk with her husband without fear of him being overheard or eavesdropped on. Maybe he could shed some light on the weird activity that had taken place that brunch, and if he knew about the meaning behind the deadly threat his wife had issued to John (though, it couldn't have been any more straightforward).

It rung out the first time he tried, so John left it awhile. He rummaged through previous reams of paperwork that were either abandoned cases or ones so totally defunct that not even the most hardboiled of gumshoes would want to crack into them. The time and energy required just didn't equate to a decent wage and way of life.

John managed to catch his client on the phone after half-past one. It was still bright outside; slanted rays of sunshine slid in through the blinds across his desk and floor, so John pulled them closed. A typical 20th Century detective environment (according to the TV and literature of that era, but without the archetypal cigarettes and booze).

"So, she threatened you?" said the client, imbuing a chuckle down the line.

"I don't like being threatened," John hit back, "even if the fee is upfront and... in cash. It's still bad for business."

"She's a harmless kitten!" The client attempted to paint his wife in an innocuous light. "She'll say what she wants to get what she wants. She's a cat with no claws! She's like her mother was, before she... passed away."

10

The pause in his dialogue was more than enough to reveal to John that this man's dreaded mother-in-law may have perished before her time. Another sleuth could fish the details of that one.

"Look, I don't care about that!" John snapped. "What about *my* protection? I have your photographs–you want them or not? Seems like you already know exactly what your *kitten* is up to, so this should make it easier in the divorce courts."

"It's not something I'm looking forward to, Mr. Dunn, especially not whilst she's running around with that gun-nut."

He had mentioned to John at the beginning, as a warning, about his wife's lover's fondness for firearms.

"This isn't the Wild West," John whipped verbal down the handset; a shaky assertion bulked up by hope rather than verified facts.

"But it is an unsavoury part of the city where we live, Mr. Dunn, and with some very disagreeable people. Tell me, did you photograph absolutely *everything*?"

"Everything?"

"Yes: his car, his house–especially the front and back doors– anything else of interest around or inside of his property?"

"It's all in the folder I have right here," John replied, almost smugly. "Each photo is high definition, checked *and* double-checked–I've missed nothing out of the brief you originally presented me. It's all there."

There was silence on the other end of the line and in the office; it contrasted with the internal atmosphere he was emotionally involved in: he was tensely being held and chewing over possible criminal activity with *future* misconduct around the corner; and yet, the sunshine continued to pollute the otherwise grey, dim weather. It was seeping through the cracks in the blinds.

They hung up shortly after, but not before John was asked to perform one last exercise in investigative photography.

***

John was back sitting outside the second last house on Clive Street later that evening, almost identical in position and timing to the reconnaissance the night before. He didn't plan on staying as late, not while Billy the Kid in there had all the potential of murder, or at least being able to just shoot him. John didn't possess any weapons–never needed them–but guns? It was as if all those black and white-filmed, chain-smoking, hard-drinking sleuths had come stumbling into his city, *his* town. That was maybe a bit O.T.T., but it didn't stop John from considering packing it all in. He didn't fancy spending his future eating his meals through a straw after a pasting, or to maximise to full effect his fears: pushing up daisies in the cemetery or in an unmarked grave.

John's trusty Nikon was charged up. The envelope containing the spoils of the previous shoot was locked away in his office. Not that they meant anything to anyone else at this time; he felt better knowing they were in his possession, whether them hidden away benefited him or not. Perhaps if shit went sour, he could offer them as bargaining chips to an interested party. There was always that in his last-ditch repertoire.

Night-time settled and the last vestiges of another beautiful pre-summer day went to bed. John prepped his camera, snapping a few shots of the house exterior whilst in the safety of his car, before quietly opening the door and exiting. He knew his client's wife was here at her lover's home–he had watched them both enter about two hours before. She had been wearing that black hat on the way to the front door, but her legs were bare. Perhaps those jewelled seam-backs were lying like flat, coiled adders in the back of her lover's BMW.

John snapped a few further shots of the garden, the garage, and the doors into the main home. But what his client wanted desperately, were photos of the inside of the home.

John went for the bold approach to begin with: he tried the backdoor. After spying through the window long enough, he was positive the lovers were upstairs. From the distances he could judge (at least, from what he could make out by looking in the window) he had ample time and space upon entering via the backdoor, and to seek adequate cover inside.

He was right on most accounts. The backdoor *was* unlocked and easy to open; upon entering, he could hear the sexual squeals and grunts from both paramours, which seemed to be coming from upstairs. At least having a floor between them would provide him with time to find the cover that was thus far eluding him.

John crept along quietly on the carpet in the hallway; the camera hung around his neck with the strap tight, to prevent the expensive device from swinging into his chest or bumping off the walls. He kept low, knees bent, back-sliding against the smooth surface, and always with one eye at the top of the stairs. It wouldn't take long for a thirsty body to come waltzing out of the bedroom up there and charge downstairs to the kitchen for a refreshment.

But wasn't that what his client had asked? For a photo of them (together or separate, or as one) in the house, preferably in the throes of passion? John had considered a telescopic camera lens and was, whilst in the car, looking at ladders on the B&Q website, should he abort the task and opt to snap from afar on a nearby rooftop.

Just as he snapped a few more flash-less shots in the living room, did he hear the unmistakable sound of an adult laughing and suddenly come bounding down the stairs. John held his breath and sunk into the room's shadows, setting his camera on standby for fear any small lights or sounds would alert the… *Christ!* The homeowner! *He* was the intruder!

A massive fish tank bubbled in the far corner opposite where John was trembling. Several fascinating specimens swam about in bliss and ignorance amid a vibrant plastic flora in their underwater domain.

John's heart continued to pound. He developed perspiration– warm, slick, beading down his cold face. His fingers tapped softly on the plastic casing of the camera, shakily feeling their way across the buttons and lens the way a blind person may do whilst reading. He was praying for a distraction or intervention of sorts.

John heard the man exit the kitchen and begin thudding along the hallway carpet, nearing the living room. His fears were confirmed when he saw the muscled, naked body of the woman's lover enter the room, his genitals swinging with each heel-first step. He heard the crunching of food and could make out a half-eaten apple in the man's hand.

John watched from the darkness as the naked man sauntered over by the settee, bent down and went elbow-deep into a holdall, where he rummaged around, eventually pulling out a small bag of white powder–now John *had* to get out! He was no stranger to a bit of the illicit (it had paid his bills for a large portion of his working life), but it was all far too close to him now. As soon as the man left, John shuffled closer to the door, straining his ears to ensure those padded footfalls ascended all the way.

When he was sure that they did, he swiftly retraced his path out the backdoor and raced to his car. On the way, the darker shade of evening, where the shadows–unusual in their gathering– seemed blacker upon his car. On any other occasion, John might have heeded this as a bad omen.

Tonight, there was no time to think.

He hopped into the vehicle and tossed the camera onto the passenger seat. Just as his key met with the ignition, he positioned his boots upon the pedals; but before he had the chance to pull out or even check his mirrors, he felt the hard barrel of a gun being shoved into the fleshiness of his cheek, while a gloved arm held his head from the other side, like improvised satin and steel components in an impulsive vice.

"Drive," ordered the woman.

***

She directed him to an empty rural car park, telling him to park the car in the furthest away space and not to make a scene and to remain seated and belted.

Once done, the car sat with its engine idle (lights off), while John–since released from her grip–could make out in the mirror (with help from the park's lighting) the client's sultry–and clearly unhinged–wife.

"Why are we here?" John asked, commanding what little strength and concentration he retained over the movement of his bowels.

The woman jammed the gun into his side.

"We'll be doing this for a long time, did you know that?"

"*Know?* Know what?"

"What we're doing! And why!"

John caught sight of her face in the mirror. The kitten had been crying. The mascara was streaming down her face like a shock rocker's stage make-up. Like that *Alice* guy...

14

"We're damned!" she said.

She chuckled, but the gun didn't lose its place. It pressed harder into John's ribs like it could then be forced right through the cage. In front, he winced.

"Damned? I don't follow. Look, the gun really isn't necessary–"

"Shut up! You've been spying on me. It's not the first time he's paid people to *spy* on me."

"Okay, all cards on the table. I'm done with it! I was going to report back to your husband tonight and tell him the deal's off."

"Whatever he paid you," she sneered, "it would never have been enough."

John fidgeted in the seat.

"Oh, it would have seen me through for a spell. Listen, can I unclip the belt? It's digging into my collarbone. Again, about the gun…"

She sunk into the back seats, withdrawing the gun from his side. That was all he could see of her apart from what he saw in the mirror: she was effectively just a gun in a gloved hand–with a voice.

"Thanks," said John after releasing the belt. "So, what's this about being damned?"

She leaned forward again, replacing the gun, though it wasn't as protruding. She would spare his ribs. She knew he had to breathe.

"Do you know what happens to you and me?"

Discouraged that she didn't take on board his peaceable approach to the weapon involvement, John decided to simply answer whatever questions the 'kitten' had in the hope it would all soon be over.

"I'm sorry, but I don't know," he offered. *Obviously, we don't fall in love!* "Do we resolve our differences, shake hands then go our separate ways?"

She didn't appreciate his humorous response. He knew this because the gun poked harder.

"We're doomed to repeat some events over and over," she told him, prosaically.

"That's nuts!" cried John. "It's stupid and impossible!"

He felt another steel jibe. *She* didn't think it was too far-fetched.

"I'm telling you, and by the time this conversation's over, you're gonna know it, too."

He could see her glancing out of the window, as if there was someone she was on the lookout for. He turned halfway to try and prise her out of the darkness with his eyes.

"Listen, let's just calm down, okay? Put away the gun–I'll drive you home, to whichever you choose. I'll phone your husband tomorrow and we can–"

"It's too late, *he's here!*"

John turned to the squealing of tyres out front. The full beam lights of the approaching vehicle weren't on, which would have alerted John sooner. The pricey Audi skidded to a halt before his used machine. And there, hunched like a madman in the driver's seat, gripping the wheel as irate as Hell beyond the windshield, was her husband.

"What do we do?" John asked her, panicking, switching his view between husband and wife.

"Don't do nothing except lock the doors. He comes across to us, he knows what'll happen next."

"Look, if this is some perverted game you two are playing, I don't want to be a part of it! Just let me go–this will all be forgotten about by tomorrow…"

"Don't you get it? You're in this with us. And there is no tomorrow, pee-eye guy."

The door of the Audi opened moments later and out stepped the significant other half of the insane couple.

"Gina, get out of there!" he yelled. He had lost a little of that maddened glaze his eyes had been displaying through the windshield when he arrived.

"Stay back, Sam," Gina warned, and this time she returned the gun to John's head. The barrel stubbed against his temple, which was coated in sweat.

"We don't have to put another through this!"

"What does he mean?" John asked, something more than panic gripping his abdomen. *Fear.* And… remembrance: her name was Gina! How had he forgotten?!

"Shut up! Listen, this isn't the end, okay? There are bad forces out there, and they don't like to let us forget our transgressions. They want us to play out our sins"–she looked down at her wedding band–"*all* of them. Until we get them right."

John tried to acquiesce with her, to say he'd believe her to the moon and back, but the drought that was setting in, in patches up and down his throat like a drying riverbed, soaked up any further efforts at talking. He felt the gun pushing harder, as if Gina wanted it literally between his ears.

"Don't shoot the P.I., Gina! *This is all on us!*"

As the two of them fidgeted in their seats, it was becoming clear that Gina was losing her nerve. The smell of the steel was more than John could handle, but before he could try at freedom, he felt the rapid heat from the blast as the bullet checked out from the searing barrel of the gun.

Everything went red, then blank.

***

The polystyrene cup of coffee left a ringed residue upon the car's dashboard under the hanging dice. Sipping the hot beverage, John caught sight of the two single pips on the foam ornaments dangling from the rear-view mirror: *Snake eyes; roll again*, he mused...

AUGUSTE (THE DARK)

Sarah maintained a friendly attitude throughout the phone interview; it later occurred to her that maybe some of the questions were thin attempts at getting to know who she was, and what she liked. But the job description was clear: *Children's entertainer required, one night only. £££.*

Sarah had experience with her nieces and nephews; had worked voluntarily in nurseries and local playgroups; she had also read *Lord of the Flies*–essayed it in that year's Higher English–but 21st Century children weren't all feral and parent-hungry. They were content with their computer games, skilfully crafting mines and fighting evil via vigilante bat-men. In this electronic hive, they secreted happiness.

It was October 30th, and it was late evening. Soon after the call, Sarah recalled the moment she spotted the advert on the cafe notice board. There was a hand-drawn map beside the text that revealed the location of the premises–an area Sarah knew well. This made her feel more at ease, for it was a prominent cul-de-sac where she suspected the residents there spoke of crime as only a myth. On a dark Halloween night, nothing could go wrong there.

The ad-owner had asked a handful of non-obtrusive questions before lingering on the personal side of what she liked to wear, and what colours she preferred. This, he quipped, was merely to do with the design and fitting of the costume itself: a prerequisite of the job. She stated–for Halloween's sake–anything in blue or red, and in a 10-12, max. The ad-owner seemed pleased and confident that the outfit he had would be more than adequate for the entertainment his children sought.

At quarter to ten, Sarah called it a night, preparing for her bed after her bath.

Anything in blue.

She lay awake for most of the next hour, as outside a full moon made of the sky its lighted stage and stole into her room in a yawning blue-white glow. Shadows fidgeted in the corners as the phone call conversation resurfaced; and as she slipped gaily into sleep, she heard the distant ringing of bells when she dreamt the words:

Or red.

***

"Clowns." That's what the shopkeeper said. "*You* got a fear of them? *Everybody* has a fear of clowns."

Sarah pressed the key lock on her phone before pocketing the device. She had been texting a friend.

"Clowns? No, not really. They're more *funny* than anything, I think."

"Hmm. Well, they unnerve *me*. It's their eyes: sad, big, like saucers; and their mouths, always smiling. Always happy, they are."

The small man tallied up Sarah's items, took her money, and handed over her change.

"There's an event on tonight," he informed her, nodding toward the window. There was an A4 poster of a Halloween party at the local community centre. "You're more than welcome. Fancy dress, if you can. But no clowns!"

Sarah took her bag off the counter. "I'm really sorry, but I've got prior commitments. Maybe if I'm home early I'll stop by. Thanks."

She took off moments after; the shopkeeper watched her pass by the window. Realising he was alone in the shop, a shiver giggled through him.

"*Funnier* than anything," he whispered, and shuddered.

***

Beep, beep! The clown on Sarah's TV was flip-flopping his way through the staged street; a rose-red horn, a squirting flower, and a long, multi-coloured handkerchief snaking out of his breast pocket were all the apparel he needed to make the studio audience laugh.

Sarah's taxi arrived at 8pm. The house, her destination, was only fifteen minutes away. The sun was dripping into the west as night stole the opportunity to pounce.

She paid the fare, exited the vehicle, and strode up the path to the ad-owner's house. The garden, bathed in early black shadow, was cut neatly; several figurines lay dispersed: Buddha, and a couple of laughing gnomes.

The doorbell chimed and Sarah heard the echoing of footsteps

19

approach the other side of the door. It opened to reveal a startlingly pretty woman, dressed in draping evening wear. She had big, beautiful gold earrings that hung low at her shoulders; a pendant around her neck with runic markings caught Sarah's eye just as the light from the hallway flashed on it.

"Sarah?" the woman asked lightly, as if surprised that the girl had arrived.

The girl smiled in acknowledgement. "Yes."

"Please, do come in. We've been waiting for you."

The woman stepped aside and motioned Sarah in. Inside was an example of elegant decorum to Sarah's eyes, with portraits of noteworthy figures, to exquisite Oriental-marked vases and other fine china. This was an antique dealer's dream, she mused.

"Come this way," instructed the woman. "I am Mrs. Sterling. My children are expecting you. We have something arranged for you to wear. I hope you don't mind dressing up for this occasion, but I understand you knew that already."

"Yes, the man explained it to me over the phone," Sarah told her, eyeing up more expensive niceties as they walked. "Was that your husband?"

"My husband?" repeated Mrs. Sterling. "Yes, him. Anyway, Charles and Kayla have had their dinner, and by the time supper rolls around we envisage your role will have been fulfilled. It really is a huge relief that you have supplied yourself this evening, Sarah. Halloween has been a focal part in our family for generations, and what better way this year to share it than with a newcomer to our tradition!"

"I'm really grateful, Mrs. Sterling," said Sarah. "I used to take my nieces and nephews out trick-or-treating. Sometimes we played indoor games so I'm sure my experiences with them will benefit us tonight."

"I hope so, too."

Mrs. Sterling stopped at a door last on the left.

"At this moment the children are preparing the room for you; may I ask that you enter here to accommodate yourself with the costume we have?"

Sarah allowed herself to enter a lit, small box-room after Mrs. Sterling ushered her in. There was a floral fragrance radiating in here, and a wardrobe older-looking than age standing in the farthest corner like a heavy, silent monster.

"When you are done please make your way through there"–Mrs. Sterling pointed to another door down the hall–"and we'll begin this year's festivities."

Sarah didn't wish to interrupt with talk of payment; instead she walked further into the room as the door closed behind her. Ahead of her the wardrobe creaked–an audible invite to inspect its innards, she mused, again.

The thick handles were warm to the touch, surprisingly. Her small fingers curled around them moments before she bit her bottom lip and pulled.

The dust was thick at the bottom of the wardrobe, as if someone had shaken it off the hanging object some time before. It lay undisturbed, settled.

Inside hung a carnival-style costume, silky, with twisting tassels dangling from the upper arms. To Sarah it looked funny in its lack of colour, in its vague design. She inspected further, gently twisting the fabric round; there was a tag sewn on, and in fading ink read *Auguste*. It meant nothing to her.

She patted the costume down, swatting any dust that remained. It was then she noticed where the floral smell emanated from. It was coming from the clown-like costume. Had it been washed prior to her arrival? Prior to the phone call? Probably. It would have been unhygienic otherwise, assuming it had been stored in the wardrobe awhile. Sarah couldn't see Mrs. Sterling, with her expensive runic necklace and styled hair, dealing with unwashed clothing.

She pulled it from the hanger, surprised at its overall length and light weight. It was a one-piece with a zip at the middle that pulled upward until it approached the neck area; thin cuffs ruffled at the end of the long sleeves, while the long legs of the suit appeared as stilts to Sarah. She had never seen a clown costume like this before. It was as if it had been poached directly from a silent horror movie.

Glancing around, she realised there were no mirrors. She would have to suit herself up without seeing the complete effect. Outside, night had arrived, and the orange streetlamps shone through the window.

Sarah perked herself up and begun slipping into the costume, careful as to not rip it. The bagginess of the lower half enabled her to slide her jeaned legs easily in; she left on her jumper, however, for it was beginning to get a bit nippy in the room. Perhaps it cost a fortune to heat such a mansion? With this extra layer Sarah wouldn't mind.

It was on. The zip stopped in its tracks under her chin; she was as snug as a bug! Or, as a clown… in a gown! She laughed a little at the thought. Tonight *was* the night of the year to induce madness, after all.

Leaning left and right, almost swaying, Sarah felt at ease within the costume. Under the light from the bulb in the centre of the room, it looked dark red; when she hopped to the window and stood in the orange glare the suit looked darker.

Opening the door, Sarah resisted the urge to call out. Mrs. Sterling had only said for her to leave the room and enter the door down the hallway. She started to walk, then found she had developed the urge to tip-toe, almost comically. Perhaps the children would be less surprised if they saw her before her grand entrance. She decided to keep quiet.

Neither Mrs. Sterling nor her husband was anywhere to be seen. Sarah looked down the hallway, to the left and right, but no sign of either adult reached her eyes or ears. Just then, she heard someone whispering from behind the wall; she moved in closer and strained her hearing.

"Is she ready?" the male voice said, audio flattened by the wall.

"She is dressing up now," said the female (Mrs. Sterling?). "It won't be long until we have her frightened out of her wits! It's always easier when they're girls. Remember that last one? She was tough. I didn't think she'd make it out…"

Sarah's eyes widened in horror as she pulled away from the wall, horrified. What was going on? Suddenly she wanted out, to run from the hallway and bolt out the front door before they knew she had heard–before they knew she was *ready*.

It must be a joke! She tried to reassure herself, convince herself that it was a misunderstanding. She pressed her head lightly against the wall and listened again.

"This has to be the last time," said the man. "That outfit surely won't last another year."

The woman seemed to agree. "Yes, I think you're right. I mean, it is getting kind of *funny*, now."

Sarah had heard enough. She turned away, preparing to quickly march out of the house when she found her way blocked by two youngsters–only, they didn't look like children. They were–dare she say it–*clowns*!? Two miniature figures with snow-white make-up and red U-shaped mouths that smiled at her. From under their small hats red hair fluffed out above their ears, like an angry cloud caught under a candle extinguisher. One of the children pointed at her.

"*Auguste, don't go!* You're our entertainment for tonight!"

Sarah backed away, nearly losing her footing on the trouser legs that took her until now to notice were dragging underneath her.

"I can't stay!" she mouthed, near whispered. The children moved in.

Just then, hands pressed against her back and shoulders, as if sensing the poor girl was about to fall.

"Sarah! Wherever are you off to?"

When the girl turned, she realised to whom the two pairs of hands belonged: Mrs. Sterling, and her husband. They too, were dressed as clowns, only their makeup was different, deliberately smeared and frenzied. With their motley-patterned hats and their hands gloved in black, their outfits long and splattered with the brightest colours, they moved forward to reach her with eager, unrelenting arms; and Sarah's shrieking and screaming tore through the house and began the fun of the night.

BLOOD DONORS

The first of thousands of blue fireballs descended from the Scottish skies sometime in late 2016, before the unforeseen eruption of Arthur's Seat in Edinburgh had liquidised most of the city and its inhabitants into molten brick-and-bone. The sleeping volcano was likely reactivated by the chemical downpour of what was first thought to be haphazard space debris, until the truth later emerged...

***

IT DOESN'T JUST RUN ON PETROL, luminous lettering on the van spelled.

Young Kenny–he was a quarter of a Century into his lifetime– spied on the blood donor van that was slowly driving down the mute street. Other eyes less keen peered through jagged, uncut hedges; peeked out from between shabby curtains in darkened houses; all seeing the same fearful four-wheeled, blood-stealing monster that was scouting in their neighbourhood. The windows of the van had been blacked out; even though they couldn't see the driver behind the wheel, the residents knew exactly what was controlling it.

The time had crept into evening, completely abandoning an uneventful afternoon, and a gang of youths–not yet feral–were clandestinely jumping from garden to garden, hedge over hedge–if it wasn't for the violence and trauma etched on their faces, it would have looked like a game–a throwback–to an earlier, happier time when the activity warranted laughter, ridicule, and a tolerance for bruised shins. Now it required stealth and caution, lest it end in death for being too casual with their discretion.

"*Sssshhh!*" one of the older kids hushed. "I can see it; it's stopped! They've not yet put the beacon on. We may only have minutes."

The small gang that he led were crouched behind him: an urban

Lord of the Flies as if written by H.G. Wells. In fact, one of the earlier 21st Century papers had headlined it exactly as that–and they weren't far off, either. Fancy that, the Scottish tabloids, independent of their English counterparts, getting it right for once.

Kenny joined them moments later from a neighbouring garden. "What's up, Kenny?" the older kid, though younger than Kenny, asked.

"Not much. You hear about last night?"

The boy shook his head.

"The rags ain't printing much these days, haven't you heard?"

"Not funny," Kenny retorted. "Anyway, the Maybury casino burnt down. Hell of a mess, too. With the airport and the trams all gone years ago, it looks like the gambling joint has also cashed in its last chip."

"The whole west side is out of bounds, is it?"

Kenny looked at him despairingly.

"I'm afraid it is, John. Quiet–they're turning around! You lot ready?"

The group that was kneeling behind them nodded in unison. Each boy carried a bag filled with all sorts: tools, pumps, antiseptic wipes, and bottled water among other medicinal things. There were even weapons: knives, clubs and a short sword. Homemade bombs and explosives in glass jars were contained in separate bags–items that were lugged around just in case.

Kenny instructed the group to divide itself across the street; one half was to carry a stinger across, whilst the group that remained with Kenny kept ready and waiting to collect the spoils. John was put in charge of the group that was to release the tyre-puncturing device. Another part of the plan was to have one of their group as a decoy–a distraction to grab the attention of the blood donor van. John selected a sprightly young boy of about thirteen without complaint; they were all receptive to his leadership, as they were to Kenny's.

The blood donor van drove back the way it came, its headlights on, dipping into shadows in the reclusive street, looking for any blood-filled meat sacks (humans). Then, the headlights caught the small running child in their path on the road: the decoy. He stopped several metres in front of the van, having run out from his hedge hiding space; the van stopped too, the engine idling and purring like a patient cat, waiting for that moment. The van shuddered into life and took off at speed, chasing after the boy.

Kenny threw a hand signal to John and his group as the van rolled by close to them; they then slid out the stinger across the unkempt road, as the wheels sunk their rubber tyres into the spikes. The front two burst with a deafening sound, like a grenade had gone off underneath the chassis of the bulky vehicle, popping the tyres loudly. The van tilted violently before crashing into a lamppost on its side. The headlights instantly died; the beacon on top was still inactive.

"Okay, go, the lot of you!" Kenny ordered.

He ran with the group as they approached the stricken blood donor van; John's team met them out on the road.

"Excellent, John," Kenny praised him. "Now, let's get the stuff before we lose it."

The *stuff* that Kenny mentioned was puddling its way out from underneath the van as they worked; thick, dark red trails of it. The boys grouped together to attach their bagged instruments to form make-shift hoses with which to suck up the leaking blood.

"It's everywhere!" one of them shouted excitedly.

"Hurry up!" John said. He was now carrying two petrol canisters. Blood dotted them on the outside. He passed them to another young man. "Here, fill these up—use the hoses, get as much as you can before they come looking."

The group rushed around the van, sucking and scooping up as much of the spilled blood as they could manage. Even though it looked directionless, they knew exactly what they were doing. It wasn't the first time they had to do this. They used a slick combination of bicycle pumps that were altered to fit half-inch hose pipes, which they could place in the liquid to draw it up into a container. It was manual work with all the hand-pumping needed; it was no *Dragon's Den* invention—it looked more like a JML product that was once seen on TV. Just a grittier version without regulation.

The boys scampered around the broken glass as they took the blood, careful not to stand on any of the shards. Medicine was a luxury now; doctors and the like were very rare. After the first invasion, much of the country's cherished hospital personnel had been systematically erased–and not just by aristocratic privatisation. Evil beings replaced them; bloodthirsty aliens.

Upon a blinking lamppost, a CCTV camera focused on the looting below. It zoomed in to capture still images of each of the group, uploading them to a computer that helped power a spacecraft on the fringes of the atmosphere.

***

Inky, oval eyes checked the data that had been uploaded to the machine's server. Despite the clear advances in otherworld technology, the screens on which they watched only threw up images in typical Earth-made format: grainy, obscure photos. There were stills of ravaged groups in East Lothian, panic-stricken at the freezing tidal waves about to devour them at Dunbar Harbour; other stills from northern Scotland, where Ben Nevis lay in a crumpled mess after the fireballs that battered into the Highlands years before. There wasn't much of the country that wasn't covered by the aliens' cameras. Wherever blood could be extracted, they sent their vans to collect it. Such priceless body oil.

Inside the spacecraft, those lidless eyes checked each scene of devastation, before happening on the chaos in Edinburgh. The blood donor van somehow knocked over and out of commission. The watcher had an idea of what had caused its demise. It had seen this unruly behaviour before.

A thin skeletal finger pressed on a transparent keypad with light-up buttons. The keypad was linked to the CCTV on Earth, in Scotland, that watched the boys clearing up the blood from the felled van. The scene on the screen in front of the being changed to the other side of the city, where another van was searching the streets. The alien was relaying a message to this vehicle: to report to the disaster area in the city and retrieve whatever was salvageable–and destroy any humans it met. A few horrid deaths to scare the survivors would be exemplary, even if it meant the loss of blood.

The message was transmitted in seconds. The van began flashing its beacon as more CCTV images and film were sent to the ship's computer.

***

They slurped up what blood they could from the crash site, leaving behind a little due to the glass fragments that had contaminated it, and ran off. There was no use staying for anything else–there would likely be another van on its way. Kenny was sure the invaders had been surveying the scene from a camera somewhere in the street.

They piled into one of the flats in Granton, barricading the door behind them. They climbed to the third-floor landing and knocked on one of the steel doors, like the kind the city council used to install if a house was vacant. Someone behind it asked for the password, which John whispered through a slot. A pair of tired, dry eyes peering through the slot agreed and opened the door for them.

"This is where you lot have been hiding all this time?" Kenny asked. He was carrying one of the blood-filled canisters, which he put down beside a battered sofa.

"It is," John told him. "For too long, maybe, but it's where we call home. We can see a lot from here. The vans, the fireballs."

Kenny patted him on the shoulder.

"You've done good, John," he praised the kid. "A lot of these buildings were destroyed over twenty years ago. Hell, we thought the only ones standing were inhabited by *them*. They liked to trick us back then, see. Hide out in the places they knew were dear to us."

A little tattered teddy sat on the sofa. Kenny spied it but decided to look away. His own loss was too much to bear.

"It's unbelievable what's happened to this country," Kenny finished.

Just then, a little girl, about nine, came out of a room. She had been sleeping or resting; her messy hair and half-open eyes said so.

"Did you get any?" she asked.

John stepped forward and tried to usher her back into the room.

"Yes, we did. There's lots of blood now. We'll fix our wounded. Now, go back to bed, Sarah."

The little girl, Sarah, smiled and noticed Kenny.

"He's new, isn't he?" she asked John.

John smiled.

"Who, him? He's been doing this a long time, baby. He helped us out there. The aliens fear people like Kenny."

Sarah clumsily walked over to Kenny; as she stumbled, he reached out, bent down and picked her up. She was as light as a feather.

"We'll never stop hiding from them, will we?"

Kenny didn't fancy frightening her with the truth, but he knew he had to make the impact soft and understandable to the child.

"Well, so long as they continue landing."

He carried her over to the window that looked over the west of Edinburgh. Fires, blackness, destroyed vehicles. There was a newspaper clipping on the windowsill. It was dated 23rd August 2016, mere months before the city melted. Kenny caught sight of it and shivered, which the girl felt being in his arms.

"Was that when they first came?" Sarah asked.

"Yes, it was. I wasn't even born then. But what a mess it made. That was such a long time ago."

He pulled the girl close, as if she were his own, and watched outside as another raging, blue fireball fell from the sky, landing near the fog-shrouded Firth of Forth. The Forth Road Bridge was a rusting structure at the bottom of the deep, and the Rail Bridge clung on to its assembly in a fractured, skeletal frame above the water.

Looking over the rooftops, Kenny could see the flashing beacons of the blood donor vans that were seeking and searching for their liquid prey, as the tell-tale sign of the blue lights washed upon decrepit building walls.

And just below him, the headline of the newspaper clipping silently wailed: ALIEN LANDINGS: WE ARE MAKING SIGNIFICANT PROGRESS!

COFFEE STAINS

1

The seconds ticked away like marching soldiers on a ceremonial parade. It was this image that brought Lisa back to the library's staffroom. She had been staring at the clock-face for two minutes' straight, lost in her thoughts; but it was now approaching ten past three. Slowly but unalterably surely, and into another Thursday afternoon.

Cathy, the head librarian, was sitting in the corner of the small room, drinking her tea and reading the latest issue of *Woman's Weekly*. Lisa caught sight of the disturbing headline on the cover as Cathy held the magazine: I LOVED MY RAPIST HUSBAND–SO I HAD HIM CONVICTED. A cold shiver rippled through Lisa then and she sighed deeply and closed her eyes. She could almost imagine being married to such a monster.

When she opened her eyes, she saw that Cathy had closed the magazine and was resting it on her lap. She was now seeking a conversation, but Lisa didn't want to talk. Not just to her; to anyone. She was tired today–exhausted–and a casual discussion about the banalities of everyday life just didn't appeal to her.

"You know the thing about these women..." Cathy started, in a matter-of-fact tone. She had pulled down her glasses and rested them on the bridge of her nose. "They're too blind to see just how fucking *evil* these men are."

Lisa tried to take in what Cathy was talking about, but it was hard. It wasn't that the topic of predatory husbands was uninteresting: Lisa had read more than her share of bad stories on that subject. It was because of those that she slept with the lights on, and sometimes with a large serrated knife under her pillow (this was only inaugurated into her nighttime routine after she had once thought that she had been followed home). Her mind often wandered, particularly on dozy afternoons, and today it was doing just that. She had used the regularity of the clock's ticking as an opportunity to daydream.

"Lisa? Do you think so?"

This time, Lisa did snap out of her somnolent state. She regretted it because she had been content in the grasp of her own reverie. But Cathy was her boss (and her friend) and it would be rude to ignore her.

"Blind, yeah, you're right."

Cathy frowned.

"It's like they *know* what's going on, but they don't do anything about it. Except this one. Look, see? She shopped the evil bastard! I would've done the same!"

Lisa smiled faintly. Perhaps it was the lack of caffeine in her system. She wasn't a heavy coffee drinker, but most days the library was quiet and there wasn't much to do but shelve returned books or reference new ones.

Cathy stood up and flipped the magazine onto the chair where she'd sat.

"Well, I'm going to head back out. I have that new order to check up on and you've got to search Bowker for that old chap's request."

"Oh yeah, I forgot about that," Lisa groaned. It was true–she had genuinely forgotten about Mr. Thomas's inquiry concerning a book published many years before. That was how tired she was.

If she had been any more forgetful, she would have thought it was a Monday.

2

Lisa stood behind the wooden desk at the counter, once again lost in thoughts. This time, however, they didn't concern clocks or soldiers. No, her distracted fascination centred on the 'horror fiction' area of the library. Few libraries separately sectioned their horror books. This genre was normally found within the fiction sector. In the library Lisa worked, the category was at the back of the building, set boldly beside the children's crèche area.

The main computer on the desk was switched on. The online screen banner flagged BOWKER, and Lisa remembered the task she had to do. She would go check out the horror books later, just to be sure they were in all the right places.

She sat down and typed her log-in information. The screen windows transformed, and she was guided to the searchable database

31

required to find the old man's book. *Out Of It All*. The book's title flashed in her mind. That was what the old guy–Mr. Thomas–had told her it was called. *Out Of It All*. Lisa hadn't asked what it was about; she only sought the usual details: the author's name and if he happened to know the date of its publication. But he knew neither.

However, Mr. Thomas did offer one piece of information to her. Through his glasses, Lisa had seen his eyes darting from left to right as if he was reluctant to share it or, perhaps, afraid? He'd leant closer to her so that his old grey duffle coat had pressed against the counter. Lisa had involuntarily shivered.

"There were only so many copies made before they withdrew it from circulation," he'd whispered.

"Made? We usually say printed. You can't even tell me the year it came out?" she had responded sullenly.

He had shaken his head, like a schoolboy retreating from a teacher's interrogative stance. Lisa had taken the title down anyway, convinced that with the help of modern technology, she would eventually be able to find the enigmatic book.

The Bowker search engine now informed her that the book did, in fact, exist, and could be obtained through various steps of 'internetual reliance' (this was a term she had coined not long after starting her assistant's job). It meant she could order it through an online seller from another website with no fuss. She scribbled down the Web address of the seller and clicked the X in the top right-hand corner of the page to close the window.

The library was quiet. Too quiet. Lisa looked along the hushed spaces between the units; long stretches of carpeted nothingness which bodies should have occupied, flicking studiously though books old and new. It was the town's only library, except for those in its school. Lisa had worked there for over two years and she liked the job. She had always liked books. She didn't appreciate the true-life accounts of murder and mayhem; like the magazines, they frightened her too much. Cathy was right. There were too many evil men in the world. But she loved being able to read and research the books that other people couldn't find. It was what made her good at the job.

Time passed. The clock said four-thirty; Cathy was outside the front door chatting on her mobile phone, so Lisa, short of work and bored to the hilt, decided on a coffee before heading home.

<u>3</u>

When Lisa got home, it was almost six o'clock. The bus journey had been horrendous, the vehicle caught in a line of immovable traffic and overfull of bad-tempered, restless humanity. There was a card on the doormat, left by the postman. He had a package for her that she'd not been in to collect and they were holding it for her at their delivery office. It said that if she called them early enough the next morning, they would send it back out that day. This was all news to her, though. She hadn't requested any packages; hadn't ordered anything online.

She put her keys on the hook on the wall and went down the hallway to the living room. She silently cursed herself for leaving the TV on when she left the house that morning (it would drain the electricity). A BBC news channel was on; a school for special needs children in Lanarkshire had employed a new crossing guard.

Lisa went into the kitchen and filled the kettle with fresh water. Another coffee was on her mind, just to help her relax from the barrage of thoughts about household chores. She lived alone, though that was no excuse for the borrowed library books that were strewn all over her flat. However, she reassured herself that *she* was clean and tidy, and her appearance attractive and well.

She returned to the living room and switched her PC on. The computer started up and she typed in her password: LIBRARY. A typically unimaginative choice, but easy enough to remember. The screen brought up her customised desktop and left it at that. Inside the machine, the cooling fan whirred.

Lisa poured her coffee and sat at the kitchen table. She flicked through that day's newspaper distractedly and wondered again about the book request from the old man–what was his name? Mr. Thomas, that was right. And the book; what was *that* called? *Out Of It All*. And Bowker had told her that it was still available.

The post office card came to her mind again, and she thought hard about what was in the package that awaited her. It may have been another sweater from her mother, knitted in time for the approaching autumn; in dark blue angora, she guessed. But then, her mother would have called to let her know it was arriving. She didn't dwell on the matter any longer.

Lisa carried the coffee to her computer desk and clicked on the Edge browser. She retrieved the scrap of paper with the Web address for the book and typed it into the browser. Within a few seconds, she received the notice: SORRY, THIS PAGE IS TEMPORARILY UNAVAILABLE. Puzzled, she refreshed the screen several times, each version being a replica of the previous page. There was no such site available, if at all. She tried Google, Bowker, repeatedly but no links appeared concerning any such book or seller. She sat back in her chair, surprised, for Bowker had listed the book earlier as being available.

<u>4</u>

When Lisa finally found what she was looking for, she was disappointed. She'd typed the title into a site's search engine, and it retrieved only one link. She was sure she had checked that one before.

The page that opened was completely black (*Not much HTML work done here*, she thought) save for one word that greeted her in the centre: ENTER. She moved the mouse pointer and clicked on it and a new page opened. It was almost the same, save for a small list of book titles on the left of the screen. Two words at the top of the screen struck her with alarm. In white lettering, they read: Suicide Titles. It chilled her. She remembered Mr. Thomas telling her that only so many of the books had been *made*. She had an idea why.

She slowly went down the list of titles, each one making her skin crawl: *Almost Dead, Crossing Over, Everlasting Darkness, Eternal Sleep*, and finally, *Out Of It All*. She felt the hairs on her arms stand on end after re-reading them. They didn't appear to be in any order. There were no author names accompanying them, either.

She highlighted the pointer over the titles, and Lisa saw that only a few were accessible. Intrigued, she clicked on one of the titles, just to see what it offered. It opened a page: SORRY, THIS

PAGE IS TEMPORARILY UNAVAILABLE. This happened with the remaining titles too, until she clicked on *Out Of It All*, where the page shifted to its destination.

Lisa had finally found what she was looking for.

***

After spending most of the evening researching the book on the new site, Lisa discovered its origins were unknown. She could find almost no trace of its background: where and when it was originally published or sold. It was as if the book had just appeared in the world of its own volition.

She was re-directed to a site after trying the seller's one again. At first, she thought that her internet connection was playing up or that maybe the seller's site had just been down during the hour and a half since she had last tried the link, but she got through this time, no problem.

The site was nicely designed, almost professional in appearance. This added credibility to it and gave her assurance purchase the book (if they stocked it, of course).

She clicked on the book title (there was no cover image available) and once again, she was disappointed. It was no longer available. Lisa felt cheated—she had come so far and had been tricked at each turn she took. She slammed her fist down onto the desk, frustrated. She wanted to smash the damn computer.

Instead, she saved the page into her Favourites folder and vowed to check again in the morning. She shut the PC down and thought it was time for sleep.

There was a vision swimming in her head, and when she hit the pillow, the haunted image began to surface.

5

In her dream, Lisa saw herself back at work, and Cathy was there, too. Oddly, so was Mr. Thomas. There was a bright sunshine coming from the windows and several kids running around in the library play area. The only unusual thing that was bewildering Lisa was the clock on the wall. It had no hands. But it was still ticking.

She was standing at her desk typing book titles at random into the Bowker website to see if they were stocked. Then Mr. Thomas approached her, again as he had in reality, and asked about *Out Of It All*. She asked him why he wanted the book and he smiled at her, remarking that he wanted, quite simply, out of it all. She typed it into the library's database and the computer displayed its reference number. She told him that it was already on the shelf.

Mr. Thomas then moved away and began searching the aisles. Lisa kept an eye on him until Cathy said (in a mumbled voice, oddly) for her to check the bins and so she left her post at the PC and walked out onto the main floor.

Mr. Thomas had found the book and was sitting cross-legged on the floor, reading each page quickly, feeding his brain with ideas of suicide. Lisa wanted to stop him, to take the book from his hands and throw it away. Then she saw him remove a knife from his pocket and place it beside him. He nodded his head approvingly of the book's crazed ideals and closed its pages. She began to run towards him, but the old man had lifted the knife and had sliced open his wrists. He waved his arms around as he sat, splashing blood across the books and library furniture like a priest soaking a possessed congregation with holy water. Some of the children in the play area looked over to him, pointing their curious fingers and watching as the crèche staff ran for the first aid box. But Mr. Thomas sat laughing; rolling onto his back, he laid his arms out to the sides and giggled wildly. Lisa reached him and fell to her knees, but he began grappling with her as she tried to restrain him.

"Don't do that, honey!" he warned. *"I'll fucking fight! It makes you this way!"*

She let him go and his head lolled backwards as his blood soaked the carpet. The kids wailed and ran for the door; Cathy quickly ushered them out as other staff grabbed the first aid box. Mr. Thomas was suddenly silenced, and the blood ceased leaking from him. Lisa looked on in horror as his arms shot up and grabbed her, pulling her over and under him. He was now on top of her, his sudden strength terrifyingly more than the rape position in which she found herself. His teeth were tobacco-yellowed and crooked. He was gurgling, choking on his own saliva.

"Get out of it all, Lisa," he snarled, spitting in her face. The blood from his wrists ran on to her blouse and she felt it trickle between her breasts. "*Out of it all!*"

And though it was just a dream, she awoke, still wanting to read it for herself.

6

The kettle clicked off and Lisa dragged herself into the kitchen to pour herself the first coffee of the day. The yawn of sunshine invited itself through her windows and she drew the curtains. Darkness. Even just for a bit.

Carrying the steaming coffee cup through to the living room, she noticed the time: 6:09am. She would leave for work in about an hour and a half, but first: the computer. She wanted to check up on the book.

As she sat down, she noted the post office card lying on the desk. She had forgotten all about the mysterious package that the mail office was holding for her. Lisa picked up the phone and dialed the office's number. It rung for a few moments before someone answered.

"Hello, south-east delivery office…"

"Uh, yes, hello," Lisa half murmured. "There's a package being held for Lisa Watson." She gave her address.

There was a brief pause.

"Yup, we have that one here. You want it out to you today? Or would you rather collect it?"

Lisa felt him pushing for the latter.

"If you could re-deliver, please…" she paused, awaiting a response, "… that would be great. Thank you."

He seemed happy enough with her decision.

"Sure, no problem. Be with you later this morning then. Hang on. There's a…" His voice trailed off.

"There's a *what?*" Lisa asked.

"Well, it's actually what there isn't! There is no return address, Miss Watson. So, you need to be in to get this today or it may get sent to our main office where it'll most likely be opened and destroyed."

A bit harsh, she thought. "I'll be home," she told him quickly, stretching over to turn on the PC.

"That's fine, then. Bye."

She hung up at the same time her PC booted into operation. The desktop wallpaper of a semi-naked pin-up greeted her, and she smiled to herself. It had been a *long* time since she'd seen a muscled body like that.

She left her computer and went to shower.

After drying and dressing, she saw that the time was now half past seven. She had spent awhile getting ready. Normally, she left for the bus at quarter to eight and it took almost forty-five minutes to get to the library, but she knew that the postman came around just after eight. Lisa had to stay at home and wait.

She didn't want her package destroyed, after all.

***

The doorbell sounded at ten past eight, and Lisa shot up off the couch to get to the door. She opened it to find the postman standing there as she had hoped. He handed a parcel over and she thanked him and closed the door.

It was a white envelope, from the feel of it padded inside with thick bubble-wrap. Her name and address were written on the front in a handwriting she did not recognise. Like the mail office employee on the phone had mentioned, there was no return address.

Lisa had telephoned Cathy and left a message on the library answering machine saying she would be in a bit later that day. She faked a sickness and diarrhoea story and hoped Cathy would fall for it.

Lisa now sat on the couch. Her TV was on and some chat-show was beginning. She muted the sound and hurriedly opened the package. She threw torn fragments of white envelope onto the coffee table and dipped her hand inside. She gripped something thick; a book, perhaps. With rising excitement, Lisa pulled at the thing and found it to be a paperback with plain black covers. *The Spinal Tap of literature*, she thought. Just black, save for the title in white on the front: *Out Of It All*.

A suicide title? she thought. This? The book was just under 400 pages and many of those were discoloured or dog-eared. There were also several overlapping brown rings that had stained the inside of the back cover. Some rings were less faint than others–more recent, perhaps.

But where had the book come from? How the hell could it have appeared? She wanted to chase after the postman to find out. Of course, he wouldn't know. And she had only been asked about it the day before. Was it possible old Mr. Thomas could have ordered it in the late afternoon and somehow known her address to have it delivered. That was possible, but it was improbable.

She thumbed through the book, riffling the chestnut-coloured pages. The text inside was small, and she realised that if she was going to read it then she would need her glasses. But, at once, she was in two minds about it: would she? Could she? The website had said it to be a book of depressing power, with the power of death concealed in its pages. Lisa desperately wanted to read the words of the esoteric novel and gain an understanding of a desire many wished to fulfil at their lowest points… like her father had once done.

She dismissed those damaging thoughts at once and concentrated on the book. Who had sent it? How could they have known? Surely Mr. Thomas had had a part in its delivery? It couldn't have been…

"… sent on its own," she mouthed, in a whisper that only the pages below could hear. And if they had, surely, they would have noted her enthusiasm, her half-hidden desperation to know the truth?

And just what would this 'truth' bring? What would it entail? What would it *envelop*? Lisa knew that there was a secret embedded deep within the heart of humanity, but only so few people could truly open their souls to receive it. And it most often played a pitiful tune, a melody of corruption that decayed proper thinking. It was a sin to take your own life but not live it if you didn't want it.

Lisa placed the book down on the table and took the torn envelope through to the kitchen rubbish bin. As she threw the contents into the bin, she reached over with her free hand and switched on the kettle.

Lisa would sit and read the book. She would consider her life, and of all the choices she had ever made. She would re-consider her options in her life and would offer them all to the words inside a book. She would wonder why books were so important to the world:

why it needed them and why they were written. After all, it was her job–her duty–as a librarian to know of the wonderment, of the fantastical and of all the direly written works. And she would wonder again why it was sent to her in the first place and by whom–and if it was truly meant for her. Lisa would take the time to consider getting out of it all.

She would also make time for one last coffee.

CRUCIFORM

1
Tease & Seize

❝Stand up.❞

The demon rose at her master's command, but at her own fidgety pace. She then saw the whip–a sex toy that he held in his frightful, lasher's grip.

The room–indeed, the whole dimension–was exquisitely new to her, and ever-so familiar to him. It was bare apart from the apparatus he had needed to conjure her: soiled ornaments, disturbing and degrading.

"You are naked."

He said it as a matter of fact, as if it was something she might not have been aware of. Her flesh was red raw from the forced transition; from being ripped from Hell's fetid womb to her birth on Earth. There was skin, and it was covered in a glutinous sludge. She was no model beauty.

"You are, too," she spoke from between blood-smeared lips. Behind those: fangs.

The smell of sulphur; her tender meat; and faeces, became the unendurable odour at this moment–of the demon's entry to his world; it was the air they breathed. She stood in a glistening pool of blood: Hell's period; urine and sweat contaminated this shimmering menstrual flow–nauseating fragrances and fluids required for the opening of the doorway that separated two worlds.

She held herself timidly, aware that his eyes were probing all over her female-like body. He was likely imagining such atrocities, such step-by-step perversities that he could inflict on her in her vulnerable position. Had Hell's surgeons spayed the creature? His own juice was incapable of supplying that all-important ingredient to create. The matter of pregnancy was not within his interests.

"What will you do with me?"

Her question excited him, angered him, to where he squeezed the sex toy harder. His cock hardened.

41

Raising his arm, he growled: "Whatever I please!"

The lash drew blood from the tear made across her cheek–it forced the demon down to her knees. She whimpered.

Her master stepped forward and lifted her head. Her eyes met with the icon of many men's destruction. He grabbed her around the back of the head.

Moments later, in the first of many aggressive thrusts, she swallowed him.

***

The ritual to bring the demon on Earth had been within his capabilities–and unsophisticated. For instance, there was no sacrificing of infants or animals; no satanic markings or chanting performed to the satisfaction of the Prince of Darkness. It seemed as if all the miscreants of Hell wanted their share of the pie, and Satan himself might have only been willing to give some of it up if it meant maintaining–retaining–order in his kingdom.

However, the thing most apparent in its ugliness was the expulsion and presentation of his body fluids. Semen, blood (like stigmata, knifed from his palms), and urine contributed to the demon's summoning; a foul trio of his essence released one-at-a-time into a wooden bowl with assorted etchings of sex positions that seemed to favour the male's view and pleasure. There was no explanation as to why these three blended body juices were obligatory to this act of summoning–it may have been a throwback to a time when civilization accepted it as some bizarre form of currency or offering. It may also have been the 'ink' Hell needed to seal the deal.

A couple hours' esoteric meditation played out in cross-legged fashion; focused, laboured breathing; and keen fondling, spurred his senses into a frenzy that attracted all but the nicest of other-worldly inquisitors. Overall, the satanic, sacrosanct ceremony lacked the romance and finesse that most movies and literature bestowed it.

It had only taken him two nights to get it right. On the first night, he had breached the doorway to what he believed to be Hell; the whisperings came fast as he sat naked and erect, permeating the walls, entering his ears. He could not familiarise himself with the language, though it sounded something old. There were many tones within the verbal draught, stirrings of seduction and traces of unpleasantness, making of the walls an invisible aperture that the words breezed through–his world interesting to whatever form of existence that lay beyond.

Moments before the whisperings intensified, when they had livened to an assortment of groaning, grunting, and growling, he tipped over the wooden bowl in fear and frustration and watched as the greasy fluid spilled over, seeping into the carpet, and staining it like a bloodied bandage. He instantly regretted his action, for the hundreds of pounds' worth of carpet was now ruined, malodorous. Why he didn't think to put down a cover or towel underneath the bowl only occurred to him afterward. He ended the ritual there and then, and the whispers withdrew.

The second night, after he had ripped up the once-expensive Persian flooring, he managed to get her to appear. Again, he enacted the word-of-mouth ritual (the meditation, the pissing and masturbating) but this time he controlled his urge to squirt, choosing instead to ejaculate at the point when the unknown verbal would become the visual.

The disembodied whisperings–male, female, and something else–filled the room for some time, and only after he shouted aloud that he would come into the bowl did the shadows break free from the corners. Undulating black figures moved around him, six or seven of them in number; swiftly segregating into double figures, a mad swarm of revolt against his heightened hesitation. His focused breathing left him hurriedly; his cock spat out its mess and it strung between his fingers like sticky icing. The shadows held back as the offering in Hell was now aware.

Then was the female creature released from the darkness to begin its deracination.

2

The Colour Red

She bathed slowly and without word in his whirlpool bath, despite every one of the adjustable jets firing at capacity like a hundred bee stings upon her body. The wound had begun to heal where the whip had broken the skin–it would leave a short scar along her cheek.

The steam from the hot water was filling the room; he opened a window to let some of it escape, inviting in the cool air from the night outside.

"About before…" he started, standing by the circular bath.

She didn't reply. Didn't acknowledge him, it seemed. Taciturn, as ever.

Her nakedness didn't fret either of them now; he had clothed after the forced oral act, but she declined a robe kept from one of his past conquests. Despite his efforts, she continued to decline, even if it was 100% luscious silk. It took him less effort to convince her to bathe.

He sat down on the edge of the bathtub. He felt inclined to stroke her hair; it was matted and thick with the viscous substance she had brought with her, but he felt that any show of affection might hinder his overall plan of dominating her. Considering her abnormal, reddish skin; eyes that defied humanity, sparkling of devilment; and flesh-tearing fangs and claws, the summoned creature could have passed for a normal woman at a considerable distance.

"It's done."

She spoke; not to him, not away from him.

"Yes, it is," he replied. "But I don't want that to come between us. What I mean is, I was caught in the event–your arrival. It… excited me. Can you forgive?"

She slowly turned her head to look at him. Her eyes were dark and peculiar; visible blood vessels obscured the sclera. Her irises; black dots, perfectly circular; perfectly staring.

"Can you?"

Her cryptic response startled him, for he had expected her to be more passive. She possessed an offset way of thinking, it seemed.

"It's within my capability," he said. "I can try. I summoned you, after all."

She washed herself while he watched. It took almost three hours–from her introduction to the human world to being towel-dried and gunk-free–for the demon to eventually occupy a seated position in his spacious living room. He had closed the door to the room upstairs–her birthing room–intending never to step foot in there again.

Their backdrop was a roaring fire, crackling and snapping in its alcove. He fed it logs and the flames leapt and writhed over them like hungry beasts.

His demonic female acquaintance sat on his Italian leather chesterfield. Since she exited the bath she had succumbed to his offer of a robe, a luxury pink silk garment with the slight fragrance of another lover. She felt disgusted that it was an item that once belonged to another woman. She took note of his gesture and accepted the robe should he force himself in her again.

"Would you like something to drink?" he asked her.

The demon thought it over.

"Perhaps a glass of fresh blood?"

"Nothing from you," she said, glancing only once his way.

Puzzled, he looked her over.

"What?" she asked. "You didn't think I would say no to blood?"

He studied her. She was going to prove more difficult to handle than he first thought.

"Well, it doesn't have to be *human* blood; there is a farm not far from here," he said.

"And you thought maybe chickens, or perhaps a tender lamb?"

"I didn't plan on anything special."

"I asked you earlier–after you had *stolen* me from my dwelling– what you were going to do with me. I wish to add that my absence will not go unnoticed. They *will* come looking."

He leaned forward, the spark in his eyes telling of his self-belief in his own invulnerability.

"I understand that you're angry," he said, "and rightfully so. But your kind…"

She glared at him as if he had offended her deeply. Her *kind*?

"Your kind," he continued, reflecting her affliction, "are like the bottom-feeders of ethereal existence. Do you know what I mean? Of course, you won't. We're all special–that we can agree on, yes? We're all made in God's image, and so on."

"And you're not scared?" she asked, with a smile. "That Hell's unstoppable beasts could be on their way now, furious that one of their own has been taken from them and abused by her captor?"

It was his turn to smile.

"That's where you're wrong, sweetheart," he said with a smirk. "I have this."

From behind his chair he pulled out a small box. The demon suddenly took notice; her bosom lifted in anticipation–or it may have been something she sensed inside the box that tempered her reaction. Whatever it was, it hadn't escaped his attention. He turned the box the right way and with his finger lifted a silver latch–the lid opened smoothly, and something inside caught the light.

"Say hi to St. Benedict, bitch!"

It was his most potent weapon against the armies of darkness. The medal inside the box, with its engraving of the Saint bearing the famous cross, was a blessed artefact that, due to the actions of the undaunted Saint, could ward off many demonic spirits. St. Benedict, never faltering when the agents of evil tested his faith, had thwarted many demonic forces with this item, and it was from this catalogue of Catholicism did the demon realise that her master intended to use it.

"Keep it away from me!" she growled.

The lid of the box remained open; the metal of the medal continuing to glint as he played with the case in his hands.

"I took this from a monk in Italy about ten years ago," he explained to her, aware that the medal was causing her some aggravation. "He said he was a descendant of Romanus of Subiaco. He maintained this pronouncement right up until he died."

"You killed him!" she hissed, cowering on the leather sofa.

"Accidentally–but you'll be able to see that, won't you? The inner eye? I doubt if Hell doesn't have its own magic mirror to witness such dreadful happenings."

"Hell doesn't miss anything!" she scolded him. "If you killed this monk and stole from him, it *will* know. The attraction lies in the damned soul of the evil-doer, not so of the act itself."

"You're quite the talker now, aren't you? Only five minutes ago, your silence was succeeding."

The demon sat back but remained frightfully aware of the medal.

"You really are a deceitful fool," she snapped.

"Bold words from the likes of you."

He closed the box hard; the cloth-lined lid produced a lively sound as it snapped shut, like rapid jaws upon their prey, and he watched the demon exhale as he freed her from her agitation.

"Tonight, you will sleep. There is a room made up—with a generous bed with expensive linen. I suggest you rest well, demon. We have much to do from tomorrow."

She glowered at him; he stood confidently, gently shaking the box in his hand as a warning to her.

"Behave, and St. Benedict remains in the box. Misbehave, and… well, we don't want to explore that alternative, do we?"

There was nothing she could do against her captor. He had taken her from Hell with the aid of the forces of black magic; from the place she existed to serve the true dark lord; this human, as competent and knowledgeable as he thought he was, was only a fickle entity in Hell's estimation.

"Just tell me one thing: what is your name?"

Before leaving her to her thoughts, he stopped at the doorway.

"I thought you would never ask!" he regaled. "And yet at the same time, I thought that you would have known."

"There's not much I don't know," she said, studying his face, "but you've masked your aura—the identification that links your soul. I'd have to rummage through your mail to know your name."

"True, there is an element of secrecy that I'm exuding; an insurance that I took from the witch doctor who divulged to me the means to excise you. If I told you everything about me, or indeed, with your powers you could just know; you would use that sensitive information against me, right?"

A smirk flitted across her face. He saw then, perhaps, a flash of her inner self, the true creature that she was, bound in Hell for eternity and existing by its scarlet doctrines; living, as it were, in the darkness, with a God who looked the other way and His subordinate keen to tempt and reward. This creature would find ways to test him.

"Mark," he said, after a moment. "My name is Mark."

She grinned.

"You began your event to take me from Hell late this afternoon, didn't you?"

Curious, he stepped back into the living room, eager to know what she was implying.

"Probably. Why is it significant?"

"Not significant, Mark," she spoke, sitting upright to stir his interest. "Are you familiar with the Bible?"

"Some of it," he told her. "It's likely all true, now I have you as proof."

"Are you baptized, Mark?"

"No."

"And are you a believer? Not just in Hell and in me; in all things, spiritual and... ethereal?"

"What are you playing at?" he growled. "Do you know something I don't? Do you think you hold something over me in an advantage?"

"Of course not, dear *Mark*," she said, sardonically.

She got up and walked over to him. For the first time that evening, she could have sworn she saw intimidation in his being as she strode.

"Read His holy book, *lest you be condemned*, Mark," was the advice the demon offered her captor.

She kissed him lightly on the cheek; there was a quiver there, she had felt it in him when her lips touched his skin–it fevered one and chilled the other. Perhaps she did know something that he didn't. If that was the case, he wouldn't give her time to conjure any tricks. Hell could very well be on its way to retrieve her, and the St. Benedict medal would need to protect him from its assault.

He grabbed her by the wrist like a battering lover; her skin was warm and smooth. He referred to the scar upon her cheek.

"The whip is always a breath away," he warned, but she didn't pull away or flinch or wince. It seemed as if she enjoyed it now.

"As is death," she replied.

"As is death," he reaffirmed.

She left his company and retreated upstairs, to the room with the well-made bed and gorgeous linen that he had prepared for her. In this room, she broke down after closing the door, throwing herself down onto the bed. He had orally raped her, used her; since that moment she was rudely awakened from her slumber–uprooted by powerful, invisible hands–he had toyed with her as if she had been any other female, human or otherwise.

Her revenge would need to be timely–with or without Hell's wicked succour.

3
A Discordant Affair

The demon woke to her master's summoning; though not a direct, verbal charge, he had taken to ringing a hand bell from somewhere in the house as if she were both maid and mistress of the manor, subservient to his needs. The sun had not yet split from the horizon, and early morning birds that had not yet broken the silence were still nesting with their hatchlings, awaiting the worms–the breakfast of their young.

Once the brass-tinged ringing stopped, she knuckled her eyes until the rubbing hurt. She was hoping that she was still asleep; in a horrid, earthly nightmare that surrounded her with the sounds, smells, and brutal touch of the world she'd only ever heard about from other demonic entities. Stories of demonic possession–of ancient rites and devil worship–were stored in the iniquitous archives of Hell.

She had not seen the sun for many, many centuries–perhaps not since the time she was thrown into the Pit in the beginning; she did not desire to glimpse at it now. She did not yearn to feel its warmth lest it remind her of a time she basked in its heat. It reminded her of Him and His Word–and something about love...

Where she was now–on the soiled Garden of Eden–there was love. It was found in many places: the heart, the mind, and the soul. It took its rightful place within Man who found many wondrous ways to both abuse and adore the affection. An untold gift from God, Mankind would surely sever its ties prematurely with its cruel, unbearable handling of love. Poets mused over it; patriots died under it. Purists in their wisdom would learn its secrets, and in their cleverness, they would realise that with love had to come its Siamese: hate. The debate rang true that love and hate needed to be experienced equally for each to be appreciated wholly.

The ringing sounded again, in the heart of the house, and the demon sat up. Mark, he had called himself (she suspected he was telling the truth), would likely be calling to her this way to assert his hold on her. It was gratuitous and demeaning–damning qualities, like smoke to her senses: foul-smelling; with unclear intention. She could not sense much in his character; her ability to see inside a human–their soul–was hidden by his knowledge and by the power of the medal he possessed. The medal was genuine; its supremacy was evident by the pain and fear she felt when he had produced it.

She rose from the bed and stepped onto the carpeted floor. Her clawed toes gripped the patterned fabric; the ruins and rustic ground on which she'd been stepping only less than twenty-four hours before felt a lifetime away.

She stood naked, her unearthly body of average earthly height, weight, and curvature; perhaps in this similarity to the ideal form of Woman he had found his desired sexual niche. Obviously, she lacked the look and substance of what an earthly woman had come to be: smouldering eyes, teardrop-shaped breasts, triangle inversé between her thighs; but he could change her if he wanted to. She could become his hand-sculpted goddess.

She slipped into last night's robe and left the room. The hallway, though milder, was as it appeared to be the night before. However, in her haste to be away from him she had not spotted the portraits and landscape paintings hanging on the walls. Now as she walked, she gazed upon each of the canvases: A Renaissance-themed military piece with a silver plaque bearing the inscription "Blasphemy from Above"; a second painting of a sun being dipped below the horizon. There was a third painting of a woman in a bedroom, in a stage of frightened undress; it scared her–it was somehow terrifyingly virginal–as if what was to follow was the vicious act of deflowering an innocent female. She couldn't explain why she felt it was a first-time intercourse. She held herself as she looked upon this painting.

"Good morning."

Mark stood atop the stairs. He was dressed smartly, casual. She looked his way, then back at the rape-fraught painting. The woman, frozen in time and terror, simply glared at something off-canvas; bra-less and with her fingers tentatively hooked into the waistband of her underwear, she didn't indicate whether she was fighting against or fleeing from her unidentified assailant.

"You like it?"

"It's hideous," she retorted.

He studied both painting and demon. In his eyes, he saw similarities between the two: one, trapped in an unknown place, watched by a powerful observer with wicked intentions at the threshold; and the other...

"I like it," he told.

"I don't doubt that you do. Such perversities attract the attention of their audiences. It ignites their seedy desires."

"Does it?"

"You know it does. Now, why the ringing of the bell? What do you have in mind for today?"

He stepped closer; a scent preceded him, inflaming her thin nostrils at the odour: citrus cut with cedarwood. It was a fresh fragrance, and musky; the scent of dew-licked logs in the morning in the mountains.

"The bell was to awaken you," he said, taking hold of the robe. He sensed her nervousness at his approach–at the way he grasped the clothing. He tugged lightly on the robe and pulled her close. His breath was clean, cool.

"I waited for hours last night," he began, whispering this, "and Hell did not show. Perhaps it still doesn't know that you're missing."

She met his eyes above hers; stone-cold and grey, his. And they told no lies.

"Hell knows," she said. "I told you before: it knows *everything*."

He spun her round so that she faced the painting; in that instant, she was the woman on the canvas, stripped and fearful, the forceful hold over her visible in her eyes and in her quiver. The most striking difference being that the monster in the real-world side was visual and in frame.

"I will get out of you what I can," he threatened. "Before anything gets near to saving you."

He pulled one of the lapels of the silk robe aside, cupping a red breast.

"And if it's by force, so be it."

He pressed against her hard enough so that she could not tilt or move her head around; if she closed her eyes or even tried to resist him it might result in some firmer punishment–the painting before them as dreaded as the picture of Dorian Gray.

He eventually loosed her, watching as she fumbled to re-cover herself. She did not cry; she did not whine or yell. In fact, her very defiance–the stubborn defence that she had constructed, whether it was in her nature or not–incensed him… drove him. Before her saviours could ride to her roaring rescue, fortified from the abyss, he would break her to find out what secrets she held, and protect anything that he could procure from that knowledge to save him from his own inevitable demise.

"Your time is limited," she warned him.

"And so is yours, so let's get on with it."

She flinched as he moved, afraid that he would grab hold of her again. He didn't; he moved around her instead, walking steadily and with intention to the bedroom doorway that she had exited.

"You want me?" she asked him, nervously.

"No, not now," he said. "There are some things in the wardrobe for you to wear. I trust they will appeal to you. They're modest items of clothing that'll suit. Wear them with pride."

He ushered her back into the room, but not before whispering into her ear as she crossed the threshold:

"This room is your province and prison. Treat it accordingly."

"You're too self-effacing," she snapped at him. "Should a woman ever see you for what you really are, I trust she'll claw out her eyes with her own fingernails."

He closed the door behind him, gradually, watchfully–like a father finished forewarning his daughter of the menace of boys and their ideas toward girls. She watched him out, too; the door closed, and she sat down on the bed.

Eyeing the wardrobe, she exhaled, then closed her eyes, and hoped that his comeuppance would come about soon.

***

A day in business is like a day in Hell, Mark heard his father say from the distance in his mind. *There is the slain, and there are those who slay. Why do you think the Grim Reaper carries that scythe? Not for swiping corn stalks. Not for fucking corn stalks at all.*

It was bravado pep-talk; Mark eventually had sussed sometime after his twenty-fifth birthday. Moronic information passed down by his father before he died on a concoction of drugs and alcohol at a business shindig in Amsterdam. Ten years blinked past miserably, in a rough memory-mash of parties, sex, drugs, *murder*...

When his travelling ended abruptly, Mark sought to look even further afield, to prise apart the border that obscured his vision of life and search for new, exciting things, said to be found in religious lore. There was always the death of the Italian monk on his conscience, however, and the stolen medal which he kept not as a sick trophy but as a possible weapon against the darkness in future.

It was all in the past. The future, with his newfound information of the afterlife and secret proof of it in his possession, would be a reward for the work he'd put in at the start. He would just need to learn to tame and nurture it, cultivate it to the point where he commanded absolute.

A day in Hell. Perhaps his father squatted there, aware now that his debauched lifestyle had been setting him up so that his one-way ticket was punched long before he went down. So what if his father knew nothing about Hell while he lived–rotting in the ground, his bones for the worms–choosing instead to live a warped ideal of Heaven. A bold image. Each man's day is due, and none is the wiser before any midnight.

Hell was real. Mark had that summed up from the many Bibles and other holy texts he had read in his lifetime, and now with the demon in his company he was beginning to know much more. She was proving quite the obedient of captives, and so long as Hell kept at bay, he would continue to pursue his longing for learning.

A day in business is like a day in Hell. The fruits of their labours!

<u>4</u>
In God We Distrust

The clothes fitted, albeit tightly; just enough to hide her true form and shape. She looked conservative, if anything hellish could ever display conformity, and only upon intense scrutiny would anyone notice she wasn't entirely human.

She met with him downstairs as he had requested. He was sitting on the chesterfield, one leg resting over the other as casual as anyone could be in his position. He held a closed pocket diary in one hand and a smartphone in the other. His jacket was slung over the back of the chesterfield.

He looked her over from where he sat, and then stood up.

"Comfortable?"

She wanted neither to reply nor return his looks but felt if it kept him from striking her or worse, then she should say something to mollify him. She felt uneasy, nauseas if anything, as if there was a gas leak that was draining her.

"In these fabrics?" she asked. "They're clingy, but clothing isn't a concern where I'm from. If it's for a trip outside, you'd better pray that no one notices."

Walking over to her, he smiled that unwavering way that made others nervous.

"There's no chance anyone will identify you." He tossed her a black beanie hat. "Wear this; you'll be well manoeuvred into the location we've been summoned. Agreed?"

"You think you're doing me a favour?"

"You're providing the favour, darling," Mark said, sneeringly. "What you are; what you can give to us–to me–is gold in a miser's hands."

She blew out her cheeks, apparently tiring of his ideals and designs, frustrated at the nonsense he was spewing. Tactics, when deployed correctly, could be advantageous to the cunning strategist; to the uninitiated hell-bent on demolition, pride would set its place in defeat.

"When do we leave?"

"There will be a car here very shortly," Mark said. He suddenly looked to the window. "In fact, it may already have arrived."

He rushed past her to see out of the window. His statement was proven. There was a car reversing into Mark's permitted parking space, the driver eager to be as close to the front door as possible– as instructed.

He grabbed his jacket from the sofa before leading her by the arm to the front door. She was now wearing the beanie hat he had provided.

"No tricks, demon," he warned her. "Your saviours are not here yet–I still hold the power."

With that, he let go of her and slipped his hand inside the inner pocket and pulled out the St. Benedict medal. She winced and held up her hand to shield her vision from it. Its presence explained her nausea.

"Get it away!" she demanded.

He returned it to his pocket.

"Now that you understand, we need to go."

Mark left the front door unlocked after he slammed it shut. He pulled the demon out into the bare morning; she smelled the green of the garden first, then the petrol fumes; but it was the sunlight that truly tripped her senses. She grimaced and gritted her teeth as the light blinded her; she was not aware of how close she was to the car, but she was hurried along as each step carried on down the path and there was no sign of slowing yet.

The driver of the car had failed to open the back passenger door for them; she heard Mark berate the man through the car's side window, calling him an idiot of some subordinate nature (the driver, she took it to be, reaffirmed his original terms of the deal: that he would not allow himself to be spotted by anyone–at least sat in the car he could be obscured) and so Mark diffused his anger by throwing open the door himself and pushing the demon inside. He too, clambered in and sat closely beside her.

"Drive," he ordered.

The demon felt the car being forced into gear before the driver nicked clutch with accelerator, staggering the motion of the vehicle, and getting it to eventually drive smoothly many yards down the road. The house behind them, that nightmare of horrors, was being pulled away. The demon looked back; she could see the house slowly diminish in size, then recede from view entirely. She felt lost. She could feel Mark's stare upon her.

"Don't worry," he said. "It's just a house. There's nothing special about it anymore."

She gazed at him pitifully. Oh, if only he had known of the full extent of her origins! That forlorn place God overlooked, where

Satan himself often over-worked. They would be trampling forth soon, perhaps even now, in their vast number, eager to bring her home. She would also ensure her captor was receptive to the punishment that they would mercilessly inflict.

Just then, she jolted in the seat. Her eyes widened as the car rumbled beneath them, as if a tremor baking in the ground had suddenly risen. Something had stolen her attention.

"What is it?" he asked her, aware of her sudden distress.

She pressed each palm against the sides of her lowered head, trying to ease the throbbing that had stricken her moments before the tremor struck. It was a painful sensation but numbing too. Massaging her temples, there was a joyous feeling that gathered alongside the soreness.

"Is it the medal? Is it working on you?" asked Mark,

In her numbed state, she somehow managed to shake her head. No, it wasn't the medal that was inflicting this stupefying pain—it was something proverbial and inspiring.

Then, it was gone.

She relaxed with ease, sinking into the seat beside him as if drunk and weary. Whatever had slipped without consent into her mind had let her know it had been there. It was a welcome violation, as oxymoronic as she could muster in her thoughts.

"Are you okay now?" Mark asked. He seemed concerned.

She blinked slowly before turning her head to meet him.

"Whatever it was, it's passed," she said, visibly showing her stupor.

This didn't seem to please him. He frowned; the driver suddenly took a sharp turn as if rounding a racetrack bend, and Mark glowered at him instead before biting his lip to stay calm.

The demon sat lethargic in the seat, but she was content that she had experienced that invasion of her mind. Something of an omen had been revealed to her; she was unaware of its true meaning at this point, but wherever the hell they were going, she was damned sure they were being followed.

***

In the corner of the bodily fluid-filled room, a robed shadow that had not been present on Earth for many centuries moved around the human waste that had been left unceremoniously on the floor; it slipped fluently between spillages of dried blood and stale semen. It left no footprints to tell of its rare visit–no extractable samples that could help pin it to the revolting scene it was inspecting. A rolled-up carpet at the side bore a stench that scented a morgue, or scenes of unbleached murder. A waste of fabric; a waste of worthy human waters.

The undulating shadow passed over the materials on the floor: a wooden bowl; traces of sweat and urine dotting the floorboards. The sacred summoning had been executed in this room, it knew. The evidence was overwhelming even if the wandering black gloom had not personally seen it performed in nearly millennia; the archives of Hell held many convincing fables that it could research to seek positives, comparisons.

One of them *had been here. The word had spread; regrettably not quickly enough, for by the time the devils reached her quarters, the demon was gone. A victim to the demands, fervour, and curiosities of Man. There likely would be punishment brought forth by the summoner; a need to study the demon, to film it or feel it or, as tales described, to* fuck *it...*

The shadow rippled and swelled with anger, trembling and pulsating its huge, soundless shape repeatedly like a black sheet caught noiselessly in a ferocious wind. It tightened the atmosphere within the room, and the room's solitary window started to vibrate. If it smashed with the ungodly pressure, there would be no one around to hear the glass breaking.

It would not wait for the human or the demon to return. In the event they would, the house could be compromised by many more of Hell's members; but if any innocents were involved and witnessed the revenge then Hell's highest-level overseers would be further displeased.

It would follow the scent left by them outside of the dwelling. The odour of immorality and impish torment would be like tracking a rainbow above a wet black and white world.

Belphegor: Lord of the Gap

The demon knew upon approaching the journey's terminus that one of the seven princes of Hell had surfaced. The inner eye distributed its forbidden images in surges and channels more complex and unnatural than Man could ever anticipate; capable of tracking its own on Earth and feeding them a volley of information to arm them during their excursion. And right now, she was feeling it; a palpable, grateful, quivering thrill; that a revered member of Hell's malevolent monarchs was in the vicinity.

The car stopped precipitously at the mouth of a quarry, skidding to the edge like a curling stone. It was as if the driver didn't know whether to drive inside or around the rock pit. Mark leaned forward and asked the driver what was wrong.

"The car," he said, shocked. "It's just cut out. Dead."

Mark urged him to try the key in the ignition again. Still no luck. The vehicle shuddered with each turn of the key, with each profane remark the driver spluttered, and Mark threw himself back in irritation.

"We'll need to get out," he said. "It's not that long a walk from here."

She looked at him, tingling, with a smile.

"Your night not working out?" she said, scornfully.

"Not yet," he said. "But there are many plans unveiled under the moon that are more frightening than mine. At least you're safe from those."

Mark pulled the handle and pushed the door out. It swung with a creaking noise that carried noisily into the air; it being the only sound present. He got out quickly; she took her time. In her lassitude, her claws ripped the fabric as she slid over the seats, and her beanie hat fell off as she erected at the side of the car.

"Jesus!" exclaimed the driver. He had exited before them and was making his way around the car, when he spotted the demon, who was now standing outside the car, hatless. Her sharp eyes and flesh-stripping fangs became his sole focus, as if she were a phenomenal, light-splashed waxwork on show.

Mark sought to reassure the driver that "it" was under his control. It was obvious to both that the driver had recognised the realness of the situation–and that unlike horror films, this demon was real.

"Just keep it away from me!" he ordered Mark.

Mark took her by the arm again.

"He's just afraid," he said, in a hushed voice. "They're not used to this kind of thing."

She ignored his comments and, linked arm in arm, set off at his pace. He wasn't forceful, but there was a creeping trepidation reverberating from his tense muscles that she felt throbbing through the borrowed clothing. He was very anxious about this trip.

There was nothing but black surrounding them; the wind blew by in whispers, tickling the hair on their bodies in agitation. Other than that soft wind the night was mute. The three of them–the driver behind the leading two–marched along a crunching gravel road, leaving the car and the quarry behind to recede just as the house had done. The night had fallen like a concrete block and they had not really noticed while inside the car.

The driver began panting behind them; he mumbled something about his heart and his inhaler, that he'd left it in the car and that he would have to go back and get it. Mark looked over his shoulder and told him to forget it, that God would see him good once they got to where they were headed. The driver relented after a few more puffs and pants and had slowed to a walking pace. Mark didn't see the need in berating him for his speed.

Ahead of them, a massive building seemed to form in the darkness–developing visibly out of it–thawing out one brick at a time. And the closer they got to it, the bigger it built itself. There were no external lights attached; the radiance from the internal ones was escaping from each window, illuminating the outside by leaking light around the edges of the window frames. This highlight allowed them to see just how tall the building was based on the ascending number of lights; there appeared, at their low level of observation, to be at least three floors of them. It seemed to be am old asylum; decrepit, unsightly, and dangerous. From the outside, the debris and materials from a past era likely remained behind those massive, muddied, crumbling walls; if the building had been disembowelled of its possessions and staff at some point in its lifetime, there were always items that devotedly remained–the things they left behind, and the ghosts of them, too.

As they stopped to admire the sight, the demon could see and hear ghostly figures wailing at the glassless rectangles which had once been proper paned windows; figures that glided as if their feet had no use being attached to their spectral torsos any longer. They bounded from empty room to empty room, everything they encountered as soulless as the bodies they used to inhabit. Ideally, it was the perfect place for the dead of an era to roam or rest.

"Well, are you happy that you've seen it?" asked Mark.

The demon looked at him.

"Seen what? There are many things here to focus on, Mark."

He looked at the building curiously.

"And you can see these things, can you? I suppose it wouldn't be too hard for you to tune into the supernatural here. There's a long, mad history about this place, did you know?"

She breathed in the crisp air.

"I had an inkling when we arrived; there are secrets buried here that would seriously affect certain privileged factions of your society. I suggest they're left unearthed. There are untold troubles lying in wait, and very restless spirits eager to instigate them."

Mark heeded the warning. He was about to urge her to continue walking when the sound of a collapsing weight thudded behind them. It was the driver.

"What happened?" Mark turned to ask him.

But there was little reply. The driver had fallen to the ground; his right arm was crossed over his chest while his hand gripped the jacket of his left arm. His face, now a dark red, tightened; his eyes squeezed shut and flew open erratically; but the rest of his body remained stiff and still.

"What's happening to him? Hey, are you okay?" Mark said.

Mark rushed back and knelt by the driver; whose breathing seemed to be going from the shallow end to the deep end simultaneously. Beads of sweat had formed above his brow, trailing down his face with each gasp of air he tried to inhale.

"Isn't it obvious?" the demon said. "He's having a cardiac arrest."

Mark glared at her.

"Well, can't you do something to save him?"

"You want me to save him? I don't do miracles, Mark. Besides, I couldn't, anyway. Not where he's going."

Mark studied both creature and human one after the other; she seemed to revel in the man's demise, watching straight-faced as he struggled with his death on the cold, hard ground. At least the demon was proof that there would be something waiting for him when he passed. The question was: what?

"Do you think he's going to Heaven, Mark?"

"For God's sake, do something, demon! Need I remind you of the power I hold? The torment I can bring with the medal?"

She knelt beside him; still without concern or compassion on her face.

"He's gone, Mark. And to where is someplace *you* don't want to be."

Mark took one last look at the driver; he had passed away as they had been arguing. His lifeless body lay while his eyes stared back glassily, devoid of the person once behind them. Mark grew angry following this show of sudden death; he grabbed her behind her neck, forcing her further down to where she was face-to-face with the new corpse.

"Look at him, you bitch! You could have done something to stop it!"

The demon tried to force her way out of the stranglehold. She slipped out of his grasp, falling to the ground on her backside. The look on Mark's face was priceless–pure gold to her. He had failed at saving the man's life, even with the threat of the St. Benedict medal, and she had let him know that. She was right in telling him that there was nothing she could have done, for she knew exactly what kind of un-Christian-like lifestyle the driver had lived. Unfortunately, it did not warrant a pass into God's kingdom.

"There was no way I could have saved him," she uttered. "He was earmarked a long time ago."

"By whom? Some big devil–"

"The *grandest* devil," she said, thus ending the conversation.

Mark accepted his defeat. He did not know the driver at all; did not even care for the man, his family, his friends. He had simply wanted to see the man survive his ailment–his heart failing–and thought that by making the demon do his bidding, someone upstairs might notice his good deed.

"We'd better move," he told her. "Can you at least do something with the body? We don't need anyone stumbling across this."

She stood up.

"My power is limited, but I can try something. It's not nice, but it's quick and works on the dead."

"Do whatever, demon. Just... get rid of him."

Mark turned away as the demon surveyed the body. He didn't wish to see what sacrilege would be performed on the corpse; what autopsy or interment she was concocting. It was better for him not to know and keep his mind on the events that were originally planned. The tall, dark building beckoned.

Through utilising perhaps Man's oldest discovery, the deceased body of their driver was aflame within moments. An unnatural, blue-streaked fire ate its way through the tough clothing and, eventually, through the meat and bones. It crackled and fed on the corpse like a hungry lion devouring its kill, leaving behind a charred mess that had the odour of a crematorium. There was minimal trace that a human being had ever been present.

"Let's go," instructed Mark.

They made it to one of the old service doors on the side of the building, just as the first drops of rain began. The weather-beaten door opened with much effort from Mark (he didn't think the demon could have managed). They hurried inside and slammed it shut. It was at this point she felt a more pressing presence, a stunning, lingering sensation that threatened her consciousness. It was an ecstasy she had not experienced in thousands of years (save for a taste of it in the car); it was comparable only to witnessing the knighting of a powerful, deserving demonic entity, or the ordaining of its human equivalent on Earth.

Belphegor, that great, cunning beast, was *here*.

Mark pulled out his mobile phone. Upon looking at it, he shoved it back into his pocket.

"Shit! No signal. Unbelievable. Well, it looks like you're my navigator now. Tell me, where are we headed?"

She looked around them. It looked like a tornado had found a way in; time had not been kind to this old place, either. A lot of the previous life of the building did remain; fragments of medical papers and instruments and supplies were scattered over the floor, some in heaps as if prepared to be lit. But it really was too dark to see much of anything else.

"Can't you conjure some fire?" asked Mark.

"Like I did outside?" she said. "It only works on the dead. Otherwise…"

"You'd have burnt me to a cinder back at the house, right?"

"How can you tell?"

"Well, there's no point standing here," he said. "We'll keep on walking–we'll be met by someone; this was pre-arranged. You didn't happen to invite anyone tonight, did you?"

The demon looked upward. The top of the building was sunk into darkness, but the power was there; Belphegor would be watching. He had eyes seeping into every scene and soul on the planet.

"I didn't invite anyone, but that doesn't mean we won't have any uninvited guests," she said. "I think we should head to the rear of the building."

Mark motioned for her to lead the way, advising that she be careful of the broken glass and other loose and dangerous items on the ground. They came to the back of the building where ahead of them a beam of light from a torch shone.

"That'll be her," said Mark.

"Her?"

"My fiancé; didn't I tell you?"

Rising anger and betrayal drowned the demon.

"You bastard!" she hissed.

"What? You thought *you* were the only one for me?"

Then, a woman's voice called out to them; to the two shifting, shuffling figures that she could make out in the dark:

"Mark? Is that you?"

"Melissa? Yes, it's me. Hold on."

"Are you alone?" Melissa shouted.

"I have it with me," he called back, "but the driver is dead."

The light stooped for a moment, then lifted.

"Never mind. Hurry up and bring it!"

Mark pushed her; the rush of anticipation evident in his shove.

The demon went along with it, shuffling forward in the dark hall like a cuffed inmate being ordered by an impatient prison guard. She followed the light his fiancé shone. A couple of times the torch was aimed at them; like a beam scanning them, before dropping to allow them to proceed untroubled.

The demon saw the torchbearer for the first time: a lithe, attractive beauty with raven-inspired hair. Mark had done extremely well to secure her affection with their engagement. It would not take this woman long to find an alternative to her current beau, if she were inclined.

"Well, well," Melissa said, excitedly. "This is a fine one, Mark."

Mark stood beside the demon.

"She was the first one to rise," he said. "The darkness did not approach with options; but we've come to understand one another now, haven't we?"

The demon glared at him.

"If you call abduction and rape an understanding, then we're crystal."

Melissa shone the torch at Mark, furious with him.

"What did it say?"

Mark sneered and found a way to answer Melissa's question without revealing any truths.

"These creatures," he began, "always the instigators. God's true mistakes. I told you before: your tricks won't work, demon."

"Ever the liar, Mark," the demon said.

Melissa punched Mark in the chest.

"How does it know your name?" she growled. "We said we wouldn't get too close."

Mark, revived from the semi-playful strike, quickly made to hush her.

"Don't worry, there's nothing she can do."

"Stop humanising it as well, Mark," Melissa told him, before stepping closer to the demon. "Your lies, fiend, is the tether that restrains you."

"Oh, really?" the demon replied, smartly. She shuffled even closer and grinned as Melissa flinched at her advance. "You'll find out very soon that it is you who will be revealed. Perhaps under that skin there is a fiend not unlike me?"

"How dare you!"

Melissa slapped the demon across the face with her free hand; the light from the torch did not illuminate the strike; the sound of the impact echoed in the darkness. Mark shivered, but found himself stepping forward, between them.

"Hey!" he shouted. "Don't hurt her."

Melissa stood back and composed herself before speaking.

"Perhaps now it will learn to not be so insolent, especially around those in charge of its fate."

The demon had by now recovered from the hit and was staring intently at Melissa.

"Your hand has pained many," the demon said, knowingly. "Pleasured most, too. *Both* sexes."

The two humans stared at one another, as if the demon had revealed a secret truth, which it undoubtedly had. In any other situation there may have followed a massive argument, an explosion of words with which to rock their relationship.

"This is water under the bridge, Mark," Melissa said. "Ignore this creature—we have to hurry and meet him."

Melissa turned and walked away from the two, using the single beam of light from the torch to light the way. Mark looked at the demon, almost apologetically; it could sense he was angry and mystified—that he had no idea of his fiancé's seemingly sordid past. He rolled his eyes and nodded Melissa's way, to which the demon followed.

They came to the mouth of another opening; without the aid of sunlight, or working fluorescent bulbs, it was hard to pinpoint exactly where they were standing, or even what the interior of the building here truly looked like. Each of them stumbled blind in the black; it would have been even more so, had Melissa not thought to bring the torch. The demon, now behind, could feel Belphegor nearby.

"Belphegor!" Melissa shouted into the darkness before them. Her voice boomed, seeming to circle them, and yet splitting off into many shadowy offshoots, seeking to be heard.

Mark, having no idea who Belphegor was, leaned forward to ask the question of Melissa.

"*Who is this Belphegor?*" Melissa imitated his query. She did so with a sneer. "He is only perhaps the most powerful demonic force in all of Hell, second to Satan, of course! Ask your prisoner if it agrees, why don't you?"

Mark turned to the demon to seek clarification. It looked at him with deep, meaningful eyes that seemed to burn out of the darkness; eyes that might have been womanly and truly female in another existence, in another time and place–but not here. Her solemn stare without smile, without scorn, hinted to him that Melissa was correct: Belphegor had indeed entered the human realm and was busying himself with humanly worries and woes.

"The medal..." whispered Mark to the demon, who in reply shook her head. Even in the shadow, Mark spotted the grin.

"Not here, against him," whispered the demon. "and it's too late to run. Follow your mistress, Mark. *She* will be your undoing."

Mark turned to once again look at Melissa–only, she had disappeared.

"Melissa?" he cried out to the black. Nothing.

The air had cooled. He took the demon by the arm and rushed ahead. Mark was suddenly reminded of where he was–and with whom–and the reality of it started to curl his skin. Not even the thought of the medal reassured him any longer, for the demon had successfully placed that doubt in his mind. It may have been powerful enough to subdue her, but if Belphegor was even more powerful...

"Melissa!" Mark called out again.

Then, the building shook as it groaned an unearthly groan; as if it were awakening from an age-old slumber and was stretching out via way of the crumbling structure. That groan–that *growl*– was not made by the creaking joints or collapsing, dusty floors–it sounded like something had gripped the building and rattled it, disturbed by the occupants inside. Mark looked to any of the available window openings but could see nothing, barely inside or out. He knew, and the demon knew: they were being watched.

"Locate Melissa!" he instructed the demon, panicking. "I need to know she's safe. Do it!"

The demon, hunched like a broken prisoner, breathed in deeply and closed its eyes, an act that mimicked a clairvoyant who is about to perform.

"What are you doing?"

The demon opened its eyes; fire burned in the black where its pupils should have been. If its head were a jack o' lantern due to the fiery glow, it may have been mistaken for a disgruntled Hessian trooper.

"I'm searching for the dead!"

Mark let go of its hand–threw it down in fright and repulsion. He could feel the heat from the flames emanating from the demon's eye sockets, warming his face and neck.

"Where is Melissa? Where is this other entity? Is she with him?"

The demon–*his* demon–projected its stare onto a nearby wall, where two loud flashes of fire sprayed from each of its eyes. The flames splashed against the brick, licking the surface with hot, lashing tongues. The demon's body had bent so that its torso went lopsided, making the eyes reach further upward, illuminating the ceiling–and the body that was twisting and falling above them, frightened and bound, was Melissa.

6

"The Prisoner Is Ours"

Mark was the first to notice, since the demon's eyes continued to burn with an intensity seen in crematorium furnaces; as his fiancé slowly spiralled head-first to the ground, struggling with her arms tied behind her back, her hair hanging distressed, she was being accompanied by a monstrous robed creature with sharpened horns protruding from its hood. The light from the grounded demon's eyes continued to pore over the descending duo, so that Mark could see that with every inch they moved the creature was slicing into Melissa's skin with its claws.

"No!" shouted Mark, but it fell on deaf, uninterested ears.

Melissa, with blood escaping from her wounds, twirled like a bloodied piñata. The creature, now grunting from within the hood that concealed its shadowed face, continued to hack away at the woman's skin, tearing away at the meat.

"Stop! Let her go!" Mark demanded, reaching inside his jacket for the St. Benedict medal. When his hand touched the box, it felt hot.

67

The fiery-eyed demon was now on its knees a few feet away. The spray of fire remained in bursts from its eyes, so that the horror that was unfolding before them from the air could be seen near its entirety.

"Is this Belphegor?" Mark asked his bowed captive.

It nodded at him. With a smile on its lighted face.

He prised open the box and ripped the medal from its holding. At that moment, Melissa's body touched the ground. She was barely breathing but still very much alive and aware. Her skin peeling and raw; her face, covered in tears and blood and dust; but her eyes–had they been a solid defence for her, they might have kept the creature at bay as she was being lowered from up high by an invisible force. They were now wide and strained, bloodshot and looking on in terror.

The creature, Belphegor, remained in the air a few feet high and away from Mark and his consort. It watched as the feeble human below paraded his metal toy in front of him, as if this was to harm this powerful, royal beast. Its robe flapped despite there being no blowing wind. Inside the crevices of the material, Mark could not see anything there.

Then, the eyes extinguished; but for some reason, a light remained. The brick wall that was the original target for the fire was scorched black and cracked, having absorbed heat hot enough to char flesh and bone.

Mark ran to Melissa. He knelt by her and lifted her up slowly. She was limp in his arms. She tried to say something but ended up mumbling bloodied spit and fear. Her eyes flitted open and shut; she was afraid to close them and yet too afraid to open them. The hovering presence of the robed demon above them; the very same entity that had snatched her up in the air a few minutes before, spinning her round and binding her with skin-cutting ties she could not see. Her arms hurt more now that they were free.

"Oh, Mark!" her voice squeezed out between breaths. "We need to get out of here! He wants to… *to*…"

Mark pulled thick strands of matted hair from her pale face.

"*Shhhh!*" he mustered, trying to console her. "I have something to protect us."

Just then, Mark was pulled away. He dropped Melissa to the

ground; she fell hard as he was swiftly removed from her side. Mark thought that it was the creature that had him. He turned and... looked at the familiar face of his female prisoner. She had returned to her former-looking self, the way she had looked that first night she ended up in his possession.

"Hello, Mark!" she hissed.

She stood naked with confidence, having removed the clothing that he had made her wear. It lay in a shredded pile in the space she had been kneeling.

"You've been rescued," Mark said. "I suppose Hell *has* been listening."

"I told you it was." She motioned over to Belphegor. "A prince, Mark. Perhaps the only time you will ever bear witness to a regal appearance."

Mark stepped back.

"Let us go." He had to throw it out there.

Belphegor's robe flapped wildly, as if the demonic entity sheathed inside was either fuming or amused at the man's hopeless remark.

"It's too late for that," the demon said to him. "He's here for both of you."

Mark looked down at Melissa's sprawled body. The shredded, bloody clothing had become her tarpaulin. Her cuts continued to bleed.

"Just take me," Mark started to insist. "Leave her alone. I'll go with you, demon."

He made to step over to Melissa, as if his standing over her dying body would be enough to thwart the intentions of either demon. Neither of the creatures moved when he did, but Mark knew that each demon was summoning something.

Mark dropped the medal; a chorus of chuckling sounded from Belphegor, although the laughter rang as if a legion of demons were huddled together inside his robe. The medal rolled away from him unnaturally as it hit the ground, eaten by the shadows.

"You won't be needing that anymore," the demon gleefully told, bringing together its hands, claw-to-claw. It moved effortlessly in the gloom that before Mark had the chance to avoid it, it was upon him menacingly.

As Melissa lay gasping her last breaths, the demon took *her* prisoner by the neck:

"Now, let's get you out of that skin!"

THE PICASSO PROJECT

1

Jonathan lay awake next to the girl. The silver moonlight infiltrated the rectangle panes of the large windows, creating obscure, geometric shapes on the whitewashed walls. A shining path started beneath the lower windowsill and slid towards the artist's easel and canvas where Jonathan had stood only three hours before.

The girl had been the subject of his current painting, a model beauty that he had encountered across town. Her height, figure, and face were perfect for his art. He would have many projects with her, he had thought as he stood at the easel, eyes taking in the classical sight before him. The girl had sat patiently for him as he painted her anew on the board, immortalising her. With Jonathan's reputation, her image would be sold in all her splendid, colourful glory to the highest bidder. The painting might be recreated and popularised; she would be *forever*, he reflected.

Turning to face the glow of the moonlit windows, he breathed easily, and he imagined. And he eventually dreamed.

2

He awoke with a start. Loud dazzling sunshine had replaced the quiet lustre of moonlight. The girl had risen early—he could hear the spattering of water from the shower in the bathroom.

He threw aside the cover and sat up. A morning cramp had insinuated itself into his legs and he rubbed them in discomfort for a few moments, before getting up. The walk across the terracotta-tiled floor felt cold underfoot. He could hear the shower water from the bathroom; the girl was clearly enjoying his hospitality.

He went into the kitchen. He opened one of the cupboards and reached in for coffee. He pulled the Nescafé jar out and placed it on the counter whilst reaching over to switch on the kettle. His calendar was pressed against the refrigerator door by a scratch art magnet—a gift from the curator at the art museum—which had been purchased not long after Jonathan's second exhibition opened. His colourful landscape visions had attracted an excitable crowd; the curator had thanked him personally afterwards, enthusing about how delighted they were with the turnout.

There was a message on the calendar that he had written for that day, *7th October, Call Neil–possible new art exhibit.* He tapped the message in acknowledgement, aiming to carry it out that afternoon. The girl would have gone by then, he assumed.

He was pouring himself a coffee at the same time she exited the bathroom. She was naked, save for a towel that barely wrapped around her body. Her tanned skin glistened from the soap; there were still beads of water running down her shoulders. The towel covered little of her chest; he could see the rising mounds of flesh where her breasts began.

"You're up early, Karen," he said as he stirred his coffee.

"I was going to wake you, but you were still sleeping, even after my alarm went off."

Jonathan picked up his cup and walked over to her.

"I do sleep quite heavy. Did you find everything you need in the bathroom?"

"I just needed freshening up," she replied, rather archly, before disappearing into the bedroom. She made a trail of watery footprints.

Jonathan turned on the TV with the remote, flicking through the channels one at a time in deliberate fashion, searching for anything decent to watch. At 9am there wasn't much but the live or repeated talk shows he hated. Put off, he clicked on the standby button and opted for the radio instead.

As he got up off the couch, the harmonious sound of the girl's singing floated from bedroom. It was an old song; Jonathan recognised it. It sounded like one his mother used to own on cassette when he was younger. He felt a need to join in but didn't. Karen probably would have cringed at the sound of his voice. Instead, he turned the radio on, rolling the dial to the first station he found. A DJ's voice trailed off as a pop song began.

Karen exited the bedroom drying her hair with a towel, now wearing only her bra and a pair of tight-fitting jogging pants.

"I'll need to be going soon," she said, twisting her hair in the towel as she dried it. "I imagine that you will be busy, but is there any chance you could take me home?"

"Yeah, sure," he replied, walking toward her. She smiled.

He got close to her, smelled the aroma of the shampoo from her hair, and kissed her. She held the towel up with one hand now, but seconds later it fell to the ground as she wrapped both her arms around his waist.

"Anything for you," he murmured, their lips parting briefly; an exhilarated nervousness in the pit of her stomach letting her know that he meant it.

3

Jonathan chose the quiet roads on the outskirts of the motorway. She sat quietly to his left as he drove the car into the estate where she lived. He didn't mind the silence, it was a peaceful one at least, but a nagging thought interrupted his calmness and he felt compelled to speak again.

"You know, I can still see you Sunday," he said.

"Yeah, whatever."

His foot played around with the accelerator and rocked the vehicle. It startled her and she glared at him.

"What the hell?" she shouted; exasperation now clear in her voice.

"Didn't we talk about this before?" he asked her directly, switching his gaze between the car mirrors and her expertly. "You knew I had other things to do; other projects to work on."

"Other women, you mean," she snapped. "And 'working on' them doesn't best describe it, does it, Jon?"

He laughed at her remark, knowing full well that she was seething.

"What can I do? I can't win with you, can I?"

She ignored him, opting to look out the window instead. But a smile was beginning to spread across her face, as if she knew she was being paranoid. She knew his painting of her meant everything to him.

He drove into her parents' driveway and turned off the ignition. The sun's brightness beat through the window and onto Karen's face, its warmth magnified by the glass. It was pleasant to feel. She turned to him.

"Are you coming in?"

"Not today," he said. "Still don't think your mother likes me!"

"It's not that she doesn't *like* you," she explained, "because she told me so. She just doesn't like what you do for a living."

"Oh, that again."

There was that awkward silence before she spoke again, using her farewell as an assurance that they were okay.

"Well, I'll let you go. Promise to call me later?"

Jon leant forward and kissed her. "Of course, I will. I have some work things to do, but I won't forget."

Karen opened the door and got out, but before she closed it, he leaned towards it and said smilingly:

"Hey, you know you worry too much."

<u>4</u>

Neil McMahon was more than just the town museum curator. Though he often travelled abroad to look for the more extravagant art pieces, Neil had, in the last few years, looked closer to home when it came to providing society with great paintings. He was an aficionado of many contemporary painters of the figurative and surrealistic styles. René Magritte had been the most influential figure in Neil's life (his own mother had suffered serious bouts of depression and may have been the primary reason of his interest in Magritte) when it came to recognising all art forms. The late Belgian's *Surprise Answer* drew from him a fierce unrelenting fixation of the unexpected–almost horrific in a way–and it was this obsession that drove Neil to seeking out and displaying fine arts. One time, on trip to Brussels, Neil had found himself discussing Magritte's work with an elderly man on the plane, and of the mystery and imagery each painting concealed. The gentleman quietly told him that, as a young man, he knew Magritte before the closure of the Galerie la Centaure, and that the painter had been a visionary to the canvas, "like the moon is to the stars", he murmured elegiacally.

Neil had found a home-grown talent whose painting he felt showed similarities to the works of Magritte. His name was

Jonathan Barr. Jonathan's paintings displayed affection for the canvas that most artists would die for. Neil had no doubts on this point. He himself had once enrolled in art college and he understood both the act and the result of the action of painting, though his talent was nowhere near as proficient as most other professional artists. It was after chance discovery of the young man's breathtaking portfolio that Neil convinced the museum board to fund Jonathan's work as soon as possible, to be taken under Neil's aegis. Eventually, the two of them became close but Neil soon found that Jonathan became distracted with girls. It seemed to him that the female sex took Jonathan's talent away from his distinctive style and resulting in bland paintings people would not pay to see. He had told this to him, but Jonathan refused to let the girls go. He would say that he needed them for inspiration and the like; he felt they drew something from him. Neil sarcastically agreed, and they argued and acted childishly. But in time, they resolved their disputes, and all was well in their professional relationship.

Now, as Neil sat in the small office in the museum, watching the staff going about their diverse activities, he contemplated Jonathan's next exhibit. It was to be another searching body of work that, if successful, would have them spoken of in every breath of art for a very long time.

<u>5</u>

Jonathan pulled off the dual carriageway into a layby and switched off the ignition. He retrieved his mobile phone from the glove compartment and began dialling.

"Hello? Neil McMahon speaking."

"Hey, Neil," greeted Jonathan, "it's Jon. How are you doing?"

"Hi Jonathan, nice to hear from you! How have you been?"

"I've been doing fine," he replied. "Nothing out the ordinary–you know me–but I've been good."

"Well, that's great," Neil said, "I'm really pleased to hear it." The opening formalities concluded, he asked in a business-like way: "What can I do for you?"

"I want to ask you about that new exhibition that's opening soon."

"The Picasso Project?"

"Yeah; is it still happening?"

There was a long pause and very quickly Jonathan had thought the worst. *They've cancelled it!* He realised that his other hand was gripping the steering wheel hard. A wave of frustration coursed through him; the unforgivable notion that the spot had been reserved for someone else seemed very real in his mind.

"It may very well be open, Jon, but to whom it's open I can't say."

"Aw, come on, Neil,' Jonathan begged, 'you know the quality of my work."

"Jon," Neil began, and Jonathan immediately noted the downward turn in Neil's voice–as if he was about to be given a lecture by the other man. "Your work is exceptional, and you know I've always thought that." Neil was equivocating.

Jonathan smiled caustically as he sat in the car. The wind wafted pleasantly in through the open window and the sun still hung high in the sky.

"Well, can you call me soon so we can discuss this in detail?" Jonathan switched the phone to the other ear. "It's just I think I could make this work. *We* could make this work."

"I'll do all I can, Jon."

"Thank you," Jonathan said. He badly wanted to be a part of the Picasso Project; he felt that it would finally 'make' him as an artist, elevate him to the top ranks.

"Just give me a little time and I'll do my best."

"Thanks, Neil. Let's make this work."

"I'll call you soon."

Jon hung up. He sat motionless in the car for several minutes, impassively regarding the road ahead.

6

The Picasso Project was not entirely new in the art world, nor would it likely ever be mainstream; the sculpting and painting of models is done year-round. The Picasso Project, however, contained a difference tantamount to the macabre; the painting of *dead bodies*.

Jonathan's fascination with the project came about after he had read about a painter on the Internet who had lost her hands in a freak car accident. Akin to the urban legend of the pianist whose hands were severed in a similar manner, it served as a painful–if not damning–reminder that we shouldn't take our limbs and talents for granted. The said painter had gone into hiding–or died. Jonathan had never been able to track her down. Nevertheless, it didn't stop his fascination with this grisly art form.

He had contacted Neil about it, but at first the curator had let the questions lie unanswered, thereafter occasionally remarking that he had never heard of such a despicable act, one that can trivialise the works currently on show at the museum. Neil closed the lid on the subject by declaring the Picasso idea 'ridiculous' and 'untrue'.

Until, Jonathan heard otherwise from a past participant.

Neil had to tell him everything he knew about the gruesome performance of painting the dead. He knew because he had studied the project, and it was what had made him aware of the possibilities of painting. That it could not only represent the living but could also be gleaned from death.

The daunting task required no more than eight participants to be in the room during a session. The depiction of death was subject to strict conditions–including dimmed lights and calming, background orchestral music playing. If there had been lighted candles upon the table in the middle of the room–instead of a cadaver–one might consider the setting romantic.

The only concern was the body. It was almost Burke and Hare-esque, except that no money changed hands, bar to the one whose painting excelled. There was a prize for the best-painted image, but that was only available to those who could stomach such a task. Many walked out prematurely, sickened by what they saw or had attempted. The misunderstanding around the project was that participants thought the body on display would be in cossetted condition and its appearance enhanced.

Often, it was not.

Car crash casualties, suicides, murder victims–there could be any form of death lying before the eager artists, and the visceral nature of the subject's demise was evident and less than piquant. The ligature bruises around the neck of a hanging victim looked ominous in deep crimson-purplish-blues, whereas the injuries of the unfortunate hit-

and-run fatality were vibrant in their reds and pinks. Death didn't always arrive in a humdrum way.

The next meeting was set to take place in a week's time. Plans were already in place to take the body before its interment.

7

Neil saw to it that Jonathan was accepted onto the project. Jonathan had trouble keeping his delight from Karen, who had been eavesdropping on most of his subsequent, congratulatory conversation with Neil on the telephone. Then a man known only as Drago rang up and gave him explicit instructions regards the venue.

"So, where are you going tonight?" Karen asked Jonathan as she lay in his arms on the bed.

Jonathan shifted the covers from his legs. Their lovemaking had been blissful and energetic and now he was sweating. The air in the room was cool. The clock on the radio said quarter to six.

"It's another session," he lied.

"Another that *I* can't come to?" she wheedled.

He looked down at her.

"This will be the last, Karen, and I promise after it you can come to *any* other that I do. But this one I have to go alone."

"But there will be others there, right?"

"Yes."

"Other artists?"

"Of course," he said, somewhat stiffly.

"Other fucking girls, Jonathan," she huffed.

Karen got up and went to the bathroom. Jonathan sighed and took it all with a pinch. He had expected this, and that was why he had bought her the necklace, a nine-carat gold ruby and diamond wishbone. It was a beautiful pendant on a slender chain.

She came out of the bathroom. In her nakedness, Jonathan began to feel aroused again, and he had already ejaculated in her several times during their lovemaking session. She was startlingly pretty.

"I have something for you," he teased.

She sat on the bed, pulling the cover over her lower body to

78

keep warm.

"What?" she quizzed, her eyes narrowing slightly.

"Close your eyes."

"Why?"

"Just do it! Now, hold out your hand. Trust me; you are going to like it!"

Karen held out her hand as Jonathan slipped his arm under the bed to pull out the box. It had been wrapped by the shop assistant and was decorated with a pink bow.

"Now, open."

She looked down at the present and smiled.

"If you think you're going to worm your way out with this, Jon..." She left the sentence hanging unfinished in the air.

Excitedly, Karen precisely unwrapped the package and carefully opened the lid of the box. The sparkling gold chain stole her gaze, but it was the ruby stone in the centre that won her heart. In an instant, she had forgotten what they had spoken about, why she had stormed off. The gift would surely tame her nerves for a bit, Jonathan thought, if not her curiosity about his work.

"It's lovely! It's beautiful!" she told him.

Jonathan lifted her chin: "*You're* beautiful."

He kissed her slowly and could feel her arms arching around his back so she wouldn't drop the box. When they were about to part, she looked at the gift again, transfixed by its charm and appearance.

"You like it, then?"

"Of course, I do, silly," she said.

He got off the bed. Looking down at the clock, Jonathan noted that it read almost six. The painting session would begin in two hours' time, and he had to be ready. In terms of equipment, that had already been set up at the location. It was the right mental state that Jonathan had to prepare for, and one that would see him through the grim task.

"I have to go soon."

"It's quite early. *This* doesn't make up for it, though." She motioned to the necklace.

"It should last, shouldn't it?" He knelt over her, his hands slipping underneath her chin. Her skin was smooth. "I mean, you love me, don't you?"

She smiled. "You know I do."

"Then this will be the last time, for a while."

"A while?"

"Yes."

"You're reminding me of the lyrics of a song I heard earlier."

"What?" he asked, curious now.

"You take my self-control."

They made love again, as the jewellery box lay untouched on the floor.

8

Jonathan dropped her off home just after seven and then made a call to Neil. The old curator told him that he wasn't going to show up at the event, but he wished him well and even asked if he wanted to change his mind.

"No," had been the answer.

"Are you sure?"

"Yes. I've waited a long time for this, Neil."

"Indeed, you have, Jonathan," Neil remarked.

After their brief telephone exchange, Jonathan drove his car to the project's chosen location–an empty warehouse on the outskirts of town. The old building's condition was as fractured as broken bones. There was a steel security shutter at every opening, save for the one that beckoned the artists. Several cars were parked outside.

After turning off his headlights to a blackening evening, Jonathan got out of his car and made his way nervously to the dimly lit entrance door and entered.

Looking into the centre of the open room, Jonathan saw where the session was being held. There were several figures shifting about in their seats, their easels in front of them; the canvas boards were as white as snow, untouched by either colour or anxiety. There was little talking–only low murmuring among the group.

He began to walk towards them when a shape on his left detached itself from the dark.

"Jonathan Barr?" said the shadowy figure in a deep voice.

"Yes, that's me."

"Who sent you?"

"Neil McMahon."

Hesitation, then:

"Good. Follow me."

Jonathan walked behind the man. When they stepped into the light, he could see that the man bore no visible menace. His complexion was surgical, skin-tight, as if he had had all kinds of surgery to renew his features. But he had the frame of an aged man, as he walked slowly and did not appear to be in good health.

"You are to be seated here, Jonathan. Neil has told me many things about you; you are a talented young man, he says."

"Yes, I've had some success," Jonathan muttered as he looked at the other artists in the circle. He could feel their eyes upon him, peeling away his outer layers. He felt uncomfortable.

"Then I hope that your talent shines through, tonight."

Jonathan was inclined to reply *I hope so, too*, but he didn't want to appear too eager to be involved in the Picasso Project, but neither did he want to seem nonchalant. He decided to display an air of cool detachment.

He sat on his stool, established it was sturdy after a few moments of shuffling about, and looked at his palette–full of paints and brushes. He could recognise the bristles on each brush–pony hair, ox hair, (perhaps even *human* hair), many kinds of synthetic filament that Jonathan had dedicated his life to learning about.

The other painters sat in the circle. Four of them staring were at Jonathan, while the others looked furtively into the shadows or concentrated with their boards. The entrance door had now been closed and barred shut. No one was getting in; effectively, without permission, no one was getting *out*.

The fresh-faced man who had led Jonathan in now returned. He stood in the circle and began speaking.

"Welcome and thank you all for undertaking this particular subject: The Picasso Project. Tonight, one very special lady–whose untimely demise we regret yet acknowledge–joins us. Gentlemen, tonight is *not* for the squeamish. Tonight–and for those who haven't yet experienced what we are about to witness–you will learn the full extent of your artistic abilities. Forget your Dali's, your da Vinci's; tonight, we are delving into a unique form of art–*your* art."

He eyed them all as he spoke, spinning slowly so that every painter could hear–no, mentally *visualise*–what it was he was saying to them. Jonathan listened and watched intently and worked out that this must have been the umpteenth time the man had made this speech. He was a professional speaker.

"So, brushes at the ready as our subject is prepared."

As he ended the speech, two men wearing executioner-like hoods pushed a stretcher into the middle of the circle. Almost all the artists were shocked and surprised not to have noticed them before. There was something concealed under the dirty white sheet upon the stretcher. Something... uneven.

"Gentlemen, your time will begin in just a minute, so let me say that it's been wonderful to see you here tonight. Good luck to you! May the best painting win!"

The two small men pulled back the cover to reveal the corpse of a murdered woman. Her body displayed numerous knife wounds, purplish slits in the skin where the blade had entered; the blood had been cleaned away, but the horrible blue colour that had replaced the naturalness of the flesh stood out, and Jonathan was sure he could feel the coldness. In fact, an icy chill ran through him seconds later–through them all. A few gasps were heard and in the sickening reality of it, a few giggles, too.

The two small men left the circle. Their host had vanished as well, without their notice. All that was left were the artists and their 'willing' subject–the corpse of a young woman, bearing the most horrendous wounds.

9

Two hours had passed. Jonathan remained at his easel, his used brushes lying on the palette beside him. He looked at the picture he had painted, wondering if there was any justice in it at all. Not just in the painting but in him, too, because that was where his passion for the art lay, not on some cold, steel stretcher several feet away. Why was he here? To impress his peers; prove something to Neil?

"Hey, buddy," someone whispered in the gloom. It was the first time someone had spoken directly to him since the session had begun.

Jonathan looked to the right. A thin balding man was *grinning* at him.

"Let me see what you've done."

Satisfied now, Jonathan gently swivelled the easel around to face the man.

"*Oooo!* That's something. You want to see what I did?"

Jonathan inwardly winced. He didn't really want to see what the guy had painted, to be honest, but right now in this place, etiquette was out the window. He would have to humour him.

The balding man swivelled his easel and Jonathan was taken aback by what he saw. The painting… it was so lifelike. The guy had carefully painted everything on his board as if he'd just taken a Polaroid shot of the body, blown up the photo and pasted it up. It was that naturalistic. In fact, it was surreal in its naturalism.

"Fantastic," Jonathan said in a hushed voice. There was other whispering going on in the circle, but he didn't want to respond, or indeed, listen. If anything, he was wanting out.

The main thing was the competition. Jonathan had almost forgotten that as he sweated over his work. All the artists were competing against one another for a coveted prize.

The host had returned. Moments later, the two male assistants from earlier came out and wheeled the body away. No talking, no noises. Just the squeaking of the stretcher's wheels.

"Gentlemen," addressed their speaker. "The Picasso Project is over. May I ask you to step away from your paintings and be seated here, please?"

He pointed to another area of the factory floor, where eight stools were positioned in an octagonal pattern. Each participant went to sit on one–from the ambient mumbling that Jonathan could make out the exchange of artistic techniques, knowledge of the great works and cited examples of creativity. These other people here with him… they had really liked what they saw.

The host who had moved them viewed each painting in critical inspection; he stroked his chin gingerly with finger and thumb, before stepping from one canvas to the next. Jonathan watched him.

After about fifteen minutes of examining the paintings, the man walked over to the small gathering. His face was one that could not dissemble, no matter how noble the cause. His eyes would perhaps water with the mysteries they had seen, his memory a pool of things eccentric. The world offered many wonders and maybe this man–whose shoes Jonathan assumed were of the finest leather, worn in by rough city strolls–had wondered them all. Standing here tonight, with these people who revelled in the bizarre, he had nothing to fear.

"I have looked carefully at what is on display," he began, studiedly giving everyone a courteous glance. "It amazes me that each year the artwork gets even more spectacular. Not one of you has failed to grasp what this project is about. Is it gruesome? Slightly. Disrespectful? No. We never mistreat our subjects. We take what is on offer because that is what this world shows *us*."

There was a thin ripple of applause from the group. Jonathan was expecting a standing ovation. He liked what the guy was saying, and he had signed up for this eagerly to be a part. The true invitation to something like this lay only with those who were maybe as every bit dead as the subject.

"It pains me to select only one winner."

There was instant attention in the room now and Jonathan felt all eyes fixed firmly on their host. Their answer, they knew, defended by his lips.

"Number four."

A man shot straight up from his stool and yelled something in a foreign language. Jonathan viewed his fellow competitor–paint-splattered dungarees dressed him; his hair was blond and straggly, with spots of paint decorating the looser strands. Jonathan guessed that he was either Swedish or German.

"A very well-done!" effused their host as he shook the artist's hand. He turned to face them all once again. "To all of you. You have all demonstrated exceptional talent tonight and these works *will* be shown to the world in the fullness of time. Thank you for understanding the nature of the Picasso Project and for keeping its secrets safe. I wish you well with the courses you choose in life and the paths you take. We are surrounded by all forms of art, gentlemen, please always be aware of that."

Disgruntled, but accepting of the outcome, the artists filtered away in minutes, leaving Jonathan the last to be seated in the darkness.

The man came over to him.

"Jonathan? Are you okay?"

The young man got up.

"Yeah. It's just…"

"Your first time, I know. No one has ever won it on their first attempt, Jonathan, if that helps."

"And why do you think that is?"

"Inexperience? Shock? I think it's a mixture of things. It took me four attempts."

"Can I ask you something?"

"Yes, but please be quick. We do need to go."

"Why did you do it? Didn't you feel sick or disturbed?"

The man smiled.

"Yes, Jonathan. After that first time, I went home thinking that I'd never go ahead with anything so demented again. The very thought of painting dead bodies repulsed me; I was sick until bile replaced the vomit!"

"Why did you return?"

"Like you, I was ambitious, top of my game. I needed something that I felt would push me over the limit, to the point where I could honestly be proud of what I had created because it was unique. This project seemed to be the only one that fitted my aspirations."

"And the police? The hospitals? No one is ever suspicious? Nothing's ever reported about… you know?" He let the question in his voice trail off.

"We have people on the inside, Jonathan, who help us out with our venture. Otherwise, we would have to resort to more brutal methods of obtaining our subjects. This has happened in the past, several times. Bodies going missing from morgues… the police sometimes arrested the wrong men… so we kept quiet. Money, Jonathan. It can buy anything."

"Even success?"

"From the Picasso Project? It's priceless. Priceless, Jonathan, because only you can decide the cost. Are you willing to make the sacrifice required to succeed?"

"I have done it before."

"Then you will pay the ultimate price, Jonathan Barr. Return and see if you can succeed. Try and try again, as they say. As *I* did. But ask yourself after you leave–why did *you* do it?"

The two men left the building, but not before the paintings were collected and packaged into a car. Jonathan helped. He got to see the other paintings and a few of them weren't as good as his; he felt cheered by this. Perhaps this was something he could succeed at.

Jonathan watched the host drive away, waving to the blacked-out vehicle as it sped into the night. He switched on his mobile phone and after a few minutes, found several text messages sent from Karen. Opening them, all they mostly told were, *I love you*.

Driving away, he rang Neil and gave him the news. He also left a request to participate in the next project. He was young, after all, and he had all the time in the world to win. He still had his exhibitions to contribute to, and there were other venues interested in his work. It wasn't the end for him, losing tonight.

If art were the competition, then so would be the trying. Again, and again and again...

THE SKELETON QUAY

The proprietor of the quayside restaurant–a resilient, moral, old man–would on occasion offer a round of free drinks to his patrons to coax them out of their shells to see what stories resident in their minds might be. Nobody seemed to want to talk about anything on *this* evening, however; but, if you were to squint your eyes through the gloom of the restaurant's bar area, then you would make out in the darkness another tough figure of moral upstanding sitting there, arms apart as if book-ending the broadsheet he was perusing. We must remember a man like this, even if he would prefer us not to.

The building had been constructed in the emerging years of the Twentieth Century. A moody ossuary, it flirts near the salivating harbour mouth–a pious entrance marker for the sea-fairing–and has done for decades; all forms of human toil and natural turmoil surrendering to its uncanny ability to remain undamaged by any element known to Man.

On the evening before the season formally poked through into summertime, the main doors of the restaurant flew open with a swiftness matched by the eager winds that rode on the tide; and in stepped a solemn eyeful: two figures together, one cuddled inscrutably inside the other's fur-trimmed jacket. The taller of the two–his mortal add-on being smaller and faceless and longer haired–marched this somewhat conjoined bulk over to a solitary booth, where the electric lamps above their heads blinked *one-two-three*, then hummed, as if gesturing to where they were to be sat. Eyes that had not set sight on visitors in ages all at once remembered their ocular obligation to pry; beer and ale rims refrained from decanting their contents into thirsty gullets as heads lifted or twisted with abrupt attentiveness to observe the new callers.

The man separated himself from his adjoined companion where they sat; it was a female who was cosied in–one could tell from the pretty features of her young, smooth face. *Beauty is power*, it was written, and this long-haired elfin girl was championing the concept with fair grace; her eyes, seeming to be crying out for sleep, could be sentinels of secrets from the way she glanced around the room. She seemed cute and intriguing, but doubtless coveted by the man who had snuggled her in.

Her acquaintance was certainly no beauty; he sat still with his big jacket on, arms as thick as trunks lumped onto the table; his hands, cultivated but haired, were gently tapping off the wood to a musical rhythm that he kept to himself. His world-weary face was book-ended by unkempt sideburns. His charge, sweet beside him; his idiosyncratic companion; he exposed one or two glances by way of the bar, to see if it were possible to grab the eye of the residing barman with a customary beckon for table service.

The lean barman, wearing a logo-emblazoned apron and fisting a small towel in the inside of a glass that he was cagily drying, proceeded to approach the two with a fraught look upon his face.

"What can I get you?"

Two drinks were asked for; not the typical beverages for this assumed pair, not a wine nor a beer, nor a slimline tonic with a wedge of lemon; not even a whisky, Scotched and on the rocks. The man plainly asked for two drinks of–

"Water?"

"Yes. In two glasses. With ice. Lots."

Bemused, the barman departed their sombre company and returned to the sanctity behind his bar. Two sparklingly-clean glasses were produced, and he sprayed into each a blast of water from the faucet. When he finished, he placed them on a circular tin tray and carried it directly back to the table. In all, it took less than a minute and a half.

"For sir..." the barman said, separately placing the glassware on the table-top, "... and madam."

With unabashed rapidity, the two strangers each grabbed their drink and gulped it down without so much as a single drop down their chins. The barman was stunned.

"Thirsty?"

The man licked then pursed his lips.

"May we have another?"

"Yes, of course."

"The cost?"

"The water here is free."

The barman retrieved their glasses and returned to behind the bar where he again filled two more and took them back to the strangers' table. They both drunk them in that thirst-stricken way seen before. The woman wiped her mouth with her sleeve, before turning to the man.

"I need more," she said in a light voice, almost a whisper.

The barman leaned over, purposely, to try and hear what she was saying.

"Is there a problem?" he asked, slyly probing. He held the tray against his body, as if it were a shield between him and them.

"No, no problem," the man answered. "Just water. More of it. And here."

He slipped his hand inside his jacket and removed an old coin from an inside pocket. He slid it over the table.

"Sir, the water is fr–" the barman set to remind him, stopping when he saw the obverse side. His blood froze at the sight of the monstrous bust that had been hammered onto the coin.

"When they see Him, they will know."

The couple heard the barman murmur the words as clear and loud as if he had screamed them out loud, but they already knew the psalm well. They had fingered variations of it in engravings of lead and copper fonts found on Babylonian tablets; in the alleged Biblical codices found hidden in Jordan some years before; and they had seen it gracing the covers of a papyrus manuscript, where the very mention of the 'Demon Star', Algol, instilled fear in the hearts of ancient Egyptians before the infant Christ was born.

"If you value your life, leave us alone, but tend to us intermittently," the man inculcated. "We just need water."

The barman, his stare affixed to the coin upon the table as he nodded slowly in acknowledgement at the man's request, remained thus. His eyes never met hers; they never met his–they were covetous in their gaze on the coin below. His right arm began to lift, and he extended his fingers unthinkingly; he was dumbly preparing to touch the coin.

The man reached out; his hands were as wide as shovelheads.

"The water, first. All night. Then, before we go, it's all yours."

And with that, he scooped up the coin in his broad hands and re-pocketed it.

The barman nodded in agreement and left the two strangers to themselves. Outside, the wind and rain became a battering force against the restaurant; it would be merciless for any fisherman to go trawling at this hour, in this weather.

The man stroked the cheek of the woman, as the weather outside intensified.

"Jacob," she said, turning from the window to face him. She was nervous–he felt her face quiver; could detect fear in her voice.

"I know, but it won't be long. Try to remain calm."

He did his best to comfort her, though he was certain his reassurance was in vain.

"It knows where we are."

Jacob pulled the woman close and cuddled her back in so that her face met with the warm, downy trim of his jacket.

"The storm is coming," she said, to him and his heart, which was drumming to a thunderous djembe rhythm.

"Miriam," Jacob said, without vacillation, "I think it's already here."

***

Remember that morally-upstanding figure with the newspaper? Like the barman earlier, he too, had seen the couple blow in; and he too, looked fretfully at their appearance, for nobody ever arrived like that without trouble gripping onto their tail. He had witnessed it before, and no doubts in his mind could ever remove the possibility he'd see it again. There was trouble brewing–trouble that carried on the haste of their arrival; he could sense it. The ominous downpour added to it, as well. But he was no seaman; had no nautical knowledge of the water, wind or tide; his time in the Special Forces had only prepared him for battles that were to be fought on land.

He stood up and took his righteous figure over to the barman, who appeared deep in thought as he sat on a stool at the edge of the bar. He wanted to probe the barman, see if there was even a morsel of information he could gather and decide for himself if any of it was threatening.

The barman–his eyes small pips, like doublets on a domino–was unaware of the approaching patron. His mind remained on the coin that the big man in the booth possessed–*somehow* possessed.

"Well?"

The advancing man had spoken to him–had broken him out of his exceptional reverie–moments before he'd sat on a stool beside him.

"Same again?" the barman reminded himself to ask.

The seated customer nodded.

"Well, since I'm here…"

Slowly removing himself from the stool, the barman returned behind the bar and began pouring from the draught tap into a new glass.

"It's here," he told the man, tilting the tumbler as the beer decanted. "In all these years I've heard the stories, I never thought that they could be true."

Perplexed, the customer asked: "What are you talking about?"

The draught stopped pouring as the barman lifted the pump handle. The glass was half empty.

"He has a coin."

"Big deal," retorted the customer, "we all have coins."

The barman placed the glass on the bar in front of the customer, in its current half-filled state. The customer picked it up and looked at it acerbically. He was not amused.

"Is this a joke?"

"Have you heard of the 'Demon Star'?" the barman spoke quietly, as if afraid he would be overheard.

The customer looked up at the couple huddled in their booth. Neither moved; they sat as if Medusa herself had turned them to stone. He lowered his head morosely.

"Aye, in the old books. It's from the Egyptian calendars, right? They keep some of them in the Historical Museum. Rome, Egypt– they all want that history purged *fast*."

The barman nodded.

"But, what's it to do with a coin?" the customer continued.

"They're in possession of one that features *his* image…"

They observed the seated couple again. Still not much movement. What if–

"It's all true. Isn't it?"

The customer fidgeted on the stool. This revelatory news had shaken him. He had expected them to be on the run from something much less tormenting than what the barman was proposing to him now. The very least, they could have been in hiding from something that was human.

"Alg–"

"*Ssshh!* Don't say the *name!*" the barman pleaded. His flailing arms almost knocked over the glass on the bar. He panicked, causing one or two upward glances to come his way. He caught their vexed eyes in the gloom.

"Sorry," said the customer, about to remove the beer glass from the barman's reach.

"No, I'm sorry. Let me get you another."

The barman emptied the contents and began refilling a new glass. Suddenly, the main entrance to the building rocked again; the wind battered an invisible succession of rams against the wood and glass so hard that everyone feared they would cave in completely during the pounding.

The customer courteously accepted the new beer that was being placed before him.

"What do we do?" he asked, reaching for the glass.

The barman, at pains now not to show his inner fear and terror, leaned on the bar.

"We sit in this godforsaken place and rarely do the old things get spoken about. Then, on a night like *this*, we get the raging weather, the rain, the–"

"Strangers?"

"–strangers, yes. Like, it's all coming together at once, for something."

"Are you sure you're not worrying over nothing? I mean, those coins can be forged, or won at fairs as prizes. I used to see a lot of tat in souks overseas–that's markets."

The barman shot upright, as if he'd been zapped by a wire.

"Come with me."

He slid out of the opening to the bar; the customer dropped off the stool and followed him to a window that was close to the front door.

"Have a look out there."

Sensing the urgency and affront that was boiling on the tip of the barman's tongue, Ronald looked out of the window, through the rain-spattered glass into the black of the encroaching night.

"What do you see out there?" asked the barman.

"Nothing unusual. It's just pissing down. I imagine the thunder and lightning isn't too far behind."

"Well, I think that's bullshit."

"Why? Wait a minute..."

"You see it now?"

"That's not right... there are too many stars... did you know that...?"

"There's not a damn cloud in the sky!"

***

The first of the berthed boats was rising on top of the tide, like proven dough before the bread oven; it knocked against the harbour wall as it bobbed and rose, which splintered the bow slightly. The boat, rapidly filling and climbing with the water level, was about to become a waterlogged juggernaut, for its mooring was compromised by the tide, leaving fate to decide how detrimental its future direction would be.

Miriam, who had briefly dropped off to sleep against Jacob's fur-lined coat, awoke with a start. She had had a dream that her unborn baby, which was safe for the moment in its placental slumber, had been offered as a gift to a faceless beast that egoistically paraded around in what appeared to be a decrepit Garden of Eden. There was the familiar tree of the knowledge of good and evil, but in this case, lengthy, twisted nooses hung from its crooked branches. The beast, a vicious-looking creature comfortable on all-fours, pranced around underneath the hanging ropes that were coiled around the branches like hemp-covered snakes (this suicidal *Book of Genesis* metaphor was not lost on her, at all).

The blackened blotch that shrouded the beast's face kept her from knowing if it was looking at her. She was present in the Garden, too, about twenty or thirty yards from the cavorting beast, but she wanted to be miles from its presence. Her belly had swollen to a plumpness not yet realised in real life, and the soft kicks that were occurring while she was hunched asleep in Jacob's bosom filtered through to her dream, so that they felt just as real. This was evident because each time she felt a kick, the beast would stop moving–as if the vile thing could feel it too.

By the time the seventh or eighth foetal kick struck her, in her dream she fell to her knees, palming the bump with one hand whilst grounding her balance with the other. She leaned back to relieve herself of the terrible pain; she could *feel* it in her dream and once or twice Jacob had felt her being unsettled against him.

The beast recognised prey when it was down. The ropes hanging on the branches of the mystical tree begun to sway one after the other. Was this God's paradise? It was just a dream, a nightmare, but Miriam could sense information being passed on to her, somehow in a telepathic way, that let her know that this place may have once existed.

"*Stay away from me!*" she scolded the beast as it pawed its way closer.

She shuffled backward; she fell onto her hands. Laying on her back, she rolled over, pulling her limp hands close to her trembling, sore body; crying tears that fell onto the grass that may have been her undug plot, the beast sprung into the air, landing only mere feet away from her. She screamed into a closing darkness as the widened, fang-filled jaws of Hell's brutal swine threatened to wrap around her like a vice.

That was the moment she awoke. Jacob had been ordering more waters from the bar, as the numerous glasses–some empty, some full–rattled against others on the table, clinking like glass instruments from the vibrations that tremored through the building.

"How long have I been out?" she asked him, reaching for a glass.

"Not long," Jacob replied. He let her go so she could adjust her position to take a drink.

Gulping down the last of the water, she could smell the food wafting through from the restaurant at the back of the building. It was a delicious aroma.

"This *is* the place?" she asked.

"It's the restaurant they talked about," Jacob told her. "I made sure. If there's bodies buried in it, we'll be safe."

"But what if there isn't? What if they rebuilt it? Any of it?"

"Then…" he trailed off, afraid to instil further dread. "We're still better off taking the chance."

Miriam spotted the barman; once or twice he had looked their way.

"Do you think the barman knows?"

"I'm sure he recognised the coin," Jacob said. "This place has history. He may know of it."

They didn't speak for a few moments; instead, allowing the sounds of the weather outside and the rehearsed movements of the barman to fill the inaudible gap.

"I had that dream again."

"Did you manage to escape from it this time?"

Miriam lowered her head, despondently. "Almost. No."

Jacob held her hand. The baby–his baby, too–*was* in danger.

"Let the coin go," she implored. "If it's what the demon wants, let it have it."

"Miriam, it's not the coin it desires. It's… it's our child it wants."

Upset, Miriam turned away from him. The rain continued to lash down; it didn't look like letting up soon. She held her belly; there were no more kicks.

***

The proprietor of the restaurant, an old, resilient and generous man, was the first to witness the carnage that befell his livelihood. From a window on the upper floor, he had spied the first boat that escaped its moorings in the overflowing harbour.

The boat that had risen highest in the harbour was looming over the harbour wall. Then, it broke free and hurtled toward the restaurant, across the carpark. Its hull rode on the overflowing water, carrying the six-meter long boat across the concrete and grass towards the restaurant.

Dumbstruck and amazed by the smooth, silent motion of the hydroplaning boat that was roaring towards the building, the owner turned to race downstairs and warn his staff and customers. In his haste, he stubbed his foot against a thick leg of a table and fell, flailing, to the hardwood floor. As his hands flapped in inept preparation to break his fall, his head smashed off the ground with such force it sent blood squirting out of each ear. It continued to trickle out of the lobes whilst his body convulsed, before death overtook.

Downstairs, a rush of cold, grey seawater flooded in through the main door, soaking the carpets and footwear in its path. The small-scale customer base stood up in unison; three or four jumped onto their tables to escape the water, while some others ran to the back of the building to outrun it.

Almost as quickly as the flood burst through the main entrance, the windows of the restaurant cracked under the pressure of the rain pushing against them. Rainwater oozed through the glass before the panes shattered. The electrics were disturbed–the lights intensified their radiance, before the bulbs died out completely. The saloon bar was engulfed in darkness. A mushy, uneasy blackness.

Miriam and Jacob didn't move. They knew what was happening. They could feel the floodwaters flowing about their legs. Chaotic scenes surrounded them: the sounds of men shouting, and chairs and tables and people being thrown as the water washed them against the walls.

The barman and his ex-army habitué had been forced to jump onto the bar, for they had tried in vain to help others who couldn't be steady on their feet on dry land, let alone ankle-deep in seawater that was inexplicably rising under them.

"It's happening!" the barman shouted, continuing to watch as the water poured in from every opening the entranceway had.

The customer, kneeling shakily on the wide bar, roared back: "What is? Not that thing with the coin? This is just a freak storm! The harbour's flooded, that's all!"

The barman shook his head. He could see stools being swept away in the flood, heavy ones that didn't wobble easily. This display of torrential rain was truly bizarre – never mind the fact there were no clouds from which it fell. And what about the boats? If they were secure in the harbour, then there should be nothing to worry–

"Watch out!"

Then suddenly, as if after an age, the front half of the boat suddenly broke through the wall of the restaurant in a drenching hail of icy water, splintered wood, and fragmented metal; it entered right on top of where Miriam and Jacob sat. It launched itself inside with such force that by the time it ended its headlong motion, the wreck was fully in the restaurant. It lay buoyed by salty papier-mâché that seconds earlier had been furniture and walls.

The wind sent serviettes swirling until they dipped into the water, where they became soggy and were washed away in the swamp; all manner of cutlery and crockery was being kicked around as everyone who had remained in the stricken eatery now scrambled to find a way out. Within minutes, it had risen until it reached the height of the bar, then over it, so that the barman–remaining marginally atop the counter–and his companion were forced off it together and into the ice-cold torrent. As the water swept the inside of the building, stripping pictures and paper off the walls, it became a killer in its wake: several bodies that had not made it out in time were floating face down, arms hopelessly outstretched, their skin pruned and purple-blue. Several other boats that had escaped the harbour also glided into the restaurant.

Soon, the emergency services arrived, but it was too late for some. The destruction was done. If nothing that had smashed was already lying dangerously on the floor, it was bobbing along the water alongside the bodies.

Outside, those who had managed to flee stood by to gawk in the pouring rain, trying to maintain their balance. They were soaked to the bone, anyway, it was impossible to get any wetter. It looked a sorry sight. The ass-ends of wrecks jutted out of the broken building.

It took less than thirty minutes for the devastation to empty the building of life. By the time help arrived, the survivors were by the carpark looking on helplessly at their nightly place of alcoholic refuge. Wondering how it all came to be so nearly destroyed, so suddenly.

The sea eventually withdrew from the harbour litres at a time, until there was hardly any water left sopping the footpaths. It sucked back into the harbour, an eager, boat-less estuary lapping up the dregs. The moon was extraordinary in the cloudless night–that spectral animation visible across the sea surface, patinaed like new silver, projected in the sky.

As the briny water retreated into the depths, the onlooker–including the barman and the Special Forces customer, who had managed to escape with minor cuts from a broken window–watched as the emergency crews raced to help. The building was immediately cordoned off, for it had started to break apart in areas. Despite its demolition, it would survive.

The barman walked around to the side, where the people-traffic was less busy. He stepped carefully over the debris that littered the grounds of the restaurant, and peered in the wrecked, wide-open hole where the first boat had entered–where the woman and man had been sitting.

There, in their booth, on the seat, were two vinyl-sized globules of diluted flesh, partially covered in clothing. One of the materials appeared to be a large jacket, with a wet, downy trim.

And beside those part-circular blobs, the barman spotted another round object; upon its face, a hammered bust of an age-old star, with an antediluvian dictum:

Dum vident eum, ut scire.

THE CUTTING GARDEN

Lucy Stevenson had planned to work her way up the career ladder long before she found herself toiling unremittingly along it. It had taken her many years, from being an aggressive tomboy to alluring tigress; from wearing football boots to fishnet tights; all along the way juggling soul-destroying employment with the Open University. When she read about training as a weather presenter at the BBC, she applied with utmost enthusiasm, and came away having successfully got the job.

But there had been a lot going on before she met with any career progress. For instance, the scandal at the start, with colleagues' malicious gossip implying that she was involved in secret meetings with senior management; once or twice she heard the gossip: that sex was tethered to her belonging. From boardroom to staffroom, Lucy had not the resolve to contain or refute the rumours. If she had been involved in promiscuous set-ups it was left behind in her teenage years. Unbeknownst to her, plans were already in place to defuse any attempts at a tribunal where misconduct–professional or sexual– would be the cause of damage to the national broadcaster's image. Instead, she fell back into her presenter role–and, by doing so, remaining on the same ladder rung for a spell–while smiling and politely informing the nation each morning of the weather from that day's bulletin.

It rained and it shined, and on some days, it shit.

***

Lucy stood naked in the bathroom on her glass Soehnle scales, filled with anticipation–but the reading was upsetting; she remained under 9st. If the digital readout had been more sensitive that morning, it could have displayed her as being a bit more on the heavier side. But it wasn't, and it didn't. No matter how hard she tried, she was still underweight.

She stepped off the scales and climbed into the shower. The hot water was soothing the muscle stress that was frequenting her body most nights. She had taken to drinking coffee in the morning, and power napping in the day. By the time evening rolled around, she would lie awake in her big double bed, alone, and wait for sleep to remove her anxieties.

She dried and dressed herself before 9am. She checked her emails from her laptop. Staff posts from the BBC (who was coming in, who was going out); some internal news about the licence fee loophole closure; and several junk emails. She never requested emails about penis enlargement, sex pills, or porn, or anything to do with online gambling; neither did she wish to send her bank details to a Nigerian with a handy Faster Payments account.

She clicked open the last read email on the list. It was from a private investigator whom she had hired to find her brother. It wasn't a kidnapping or a missing persons' case–Paul had simply moved years before but hadn't bothered to tell his family to where. It was lucky for Lucy that she had him tracked down when she did, for the siblings' surviving parent was in no shape to go searching for his missing son.

The email contained the basics: who, what, why, where, and *"When am I getting paid the balance, Miss Stevenson?"* She ignored that last bit, concerned more about Paul and where he was living than the P.I.'s fee. Besides, the salary for a weather presenter more than covered what the private investigator was charging. Maybe he was a little too steep (unapologetically citing numerous overheads, fuel and meal relief for the long hours) but Lucy was sure he no doubt had each finger in some kind of pie.

The rest of the email detailed the information she needed. It was all there: her brother, and where he now worked. It appeared he had given up on the bucolic surroundings that was his childhood and was now rooted in the heart of the Merchant City: from where Lucy lived, Glasgow was only an hour or so away.

Lucy ran over the details again and again and even recalled the phone conversation that she had had with the P.I. some hours after the email had appeared in her email inbox.

"You know how to get there?" the P.I. asked.

Lucy, who had not long finished work at the studio, replied:

"Yes, I've passed through the city before. You're sure he's

there?"

"I sent you the photo attachments."

But Lucy hadn't seen her brother in years, and the badly focused photos she'd been sent could have been anyone with sunglasses on. Yet, there was something in the man's face that reminded her of Paul; a pose in one of the snapshots reminiscent of the way he looked as a child. *A child.*

"It must be him, Miss Stevenson. I checked everywhere possible: government records, building and property applications. There are no death records in his name, either–funny, that. We've all got a namesake somewhere. If he's alive then it's him in the photos, and it's him running that club. Oh, and do you have the remaining fee *in cash...*"

That club. That's what the P.I. had called it. He was right. Google Maps confirmed it for her. Her younger brother owned a strip club in the city. That apple seemed to have fallen *very* far from the tree.

Lucy exited her email. She folded the laptop lid and sat impassively regarding the neatness, shape, and view of her living room. *Paul would have something to say about a place like this,* she thought. From the limited space and furnishings that they both grew up in, this seemed like a paradise: huge wall-mounted flat screen TV; frosted, nested glass tables, plus many other trinkets and ornaments. It wasn't chic, but it sure wasn't shabby.

Lucy left her upmarket flat, on the periphery of the upmarket city, and joined the motorway. She could count on both hands the number of years that she hadn't seen her brother. Their father was ill, their mother already dead. But what bugged her most was that Paul himself hadn't sought her out all these years–and she wanted to know why.

There was something in her blood telling her so.

***

In the living room, there is an eight-year old girl with jeans faded at the knees, and proudly sporting a T-shirt bearing the logo Optimus Prime *yelling a space war-cry; beside her, her younger brother is sitting eagerly with pencils and paper, drawing what he thinks is a representation of dinosaurs and prehistoric volcanoes and brightly-*

coloured foliage. He thinks there should be a sea in there too but can't quite decide which dinosaur is better at swimming.

The girl tosses a soft ball at him, but the boy rolls it away from his masterpiece. He's afraid the distraction will cause him to lose focus. But he doesn't berate his big sister. She's only playing.

"Come on, Paul," she says, "throw it back!"

The boy finishes a pterodactyl that's been drawn centimetres from the reach of a ravenous Tyrannosaurus rex.

"Wait until I'm finished, Lucy," he says, colouring in.

Lucy, with the worn jeans, now watches the TV with interest. A computerised rendering of the UK is onscreen, and it's covered in numbers and black wavy lines, with little suns and clouds and lightning bolts at various points (although she didn't quite understand what she was seeing then, the graphics and fretting presenter indicated something rough was happening down south).

"I'm going to be on telly one day," Lucy says.

Paul stops drawing and notices what she is watching.

"You mean, in there?"

"Not in it, silly," she says. "Telling the weather."

"Telling it what?" Paul asks.

"That it's going to be rainy and sunny all over," Lucy replies.

"Maybe you could do that? I hate when it rains," Paul finishes, and resumes his colouring.

Their dad is having a nap on the couch beside them while their mother is finishing a pile of ironing in the kitchen. Outside, growling thunderclouds are dividing the sky ...

***

Lucy decided to visit her father first. She exited the M8 close to junction five, and proceeded to drive to the small town that she grew up in. The smell of fertiliser was in the air; it smelt sufficiently foul and rotten-egged enough to make her increase the air-con to blast the pine Febreze vent freshener. It wouldn't take long for the egg-smell to dissipate.

She drove to the end of a long road toward her father's house. She knew this street blindfolded; could approach each gate along the pavement with her hands pocketed. Paul and she had jumped over every hedge, had skipped over every crack on the footpath, climbed every tree in the neighbouring gardens. And it wasn't that long ago–twenty years or so, double figures in terms of numbers. But in terms of years, it was twenty times three hundred and sixty-five.

She parked the car outside her father's house. It looked old from the outside. There was nothing spectacular about the council home–it only reflected the aged signs of the workmanship that had gone into building it in the sixties. Many of those builders would be in their eighties by now. Maybe even passed on. The housing stock that lined every street was their communal legacy.

She walked up the path, eyeing the garden. Daisies had sprung up on the lawn and spread inequitably among the grass; there were dandelion blossoms and buttercups dotted about, too. Her dad liked to see gardens like that. Her parents once cultivated an area in their garden in the earlier years and had planted many flowers for indoor decoration. It was mainly her mother's hobby, with her father's labour. Lucy had grown used to the scented flowers and foliage. Whenever and wherever she smelt them again, it always brought her back to her youth.

She tried the door handle first, but it was locked. She knocked and waited for a time, before walking to the front room window. She looked in through the netting obscuring the interior but couldn't make out the shape of her dad inside.

"You looking for Ron?"

Startled, Lucy stepped back from the window. There was a man wearing a charcoal-coloured flat cap, standing in the next garden; he could have been her father's age, maybe older; she hadn't known him as a neighbour while she was growing up.

"My dad, yes," she said.

The man seemed surprised.

"He never told me he had such a beautiful young woman for a daughter!"

Lucy, embarrassed, looked down at her boots. The 'biker chick' look was stylish, though she didn't own a motorbike and didn't think she ever would. But the boots looked cool.

"Do you know where he is?" she asked him.

Flat Cap looked at the house, then back at Lucy.

"No," he said without conviction. "I mean, there was an

ambulance parked in the street here this morning, but I don't think it was for him–you would've known that by now, I suppose. Ron usually accompanies the old dear down the road as she walks her dog–it's an annoying little shit–excuse my language, please. They shouldn't be long, I imagine."

Lucy returned to the garden path.

"I'll come back later, then," she said. "But if you happen to see him sooner, please let him know I was here."

"Will do," Flat Cap promised. He turned and went into the house preceding the garden in which he'd stood.

A little discontented, Lucy returned to her car thinking she had maybe missed her father as he went out on his jaunt with the old woman and her dog. She would hopefully catch him on her way home.

**

The slip-roads off the motorway into Glasgow were like arteries in the body–so many of them, and all leading to a blood-pumping centre.

Lucy saw the exit for Charing Cross and took it. She would use her Sat-Nav to navigate through the city and find the location of Paul's club. The P.I. had suggested she would find her brother there. She didn't question the sleuth–she just had faith in her money delivering the correct intelligence.

She pulled into a cobblestoned street. There were bistros and bookmakers down each side; there were perhaps a couple of casinos, too, from the look of the tinted windows with fruit machine decals and blinking lights.

Lucy idled outside the entrance to a car park before spying an available space. She drove in and parked, then found the ticket machine and inserted the correct coinage for up to three hours' stay. She had foreseen this requirement and made sure that she was carrying several pound coins in her jacket pocket. The slip printed and was ejected from the machine; she took it and walked back to the car to place it on the dashboard. She had no idea how long she would be in the club but figured three hours was adequate.

Lucy walked unstably across the cobblestone street. Nancy Sinatra's *These Boots Are Made for Walkin'* played in her mind, serving only to increase the comic effect if she were to twist an ankle and stumble (it wouldn't be funny for *her*, but probably to some of the other people that were walking by). She eventually entered the tumult of the city centre, where the ants of humanity dashed by her with their designer shopping bags and food cartons. She neither favoured nor fancied the fast-food eateries of the urban setting; Lucy preferred the serene environment that her local restaurants were proud to have instituted, and some that often were child-free in their clientele, making of an evening's dining as palliative as eating on a tranquil ocean cruise.

She carried on walking, keeping to the edge where the shop entrances met the pavement. She didn't want to get caught up in the rush. She had to keep her eyes on finding the strip club. She wasn't sure how a place like that would advertise, though. Did it have a sign outside the building? Advertising boards; or flyers in a phone box? Maybe it would be less obvious in its promotion, to eliminate the embarrassment felt by neighbouring properties.

But there it was. Lucy spotted the club on the other side of the busy road; there was a banner above the doorway that announced it, a printed, lissom silhouette of a woman twisted around a dance pole like a snake that has coiled around its immobilised prey. There was nothing pleasant nor overly-offensive about the club's façade–it was the way it was designed to be; the doorman standing with his Bluetooth earpiece in only made it seem less amiable, if anything, but safer and stricter against those harbouring a more hands-on approach to the dancers. And the club name? *The Cutting Garden.*

Lucy crossed the busy street through a deluge of bodies that flew past either side of her. She maintained her pace and continued to the club's doorway. The doorman, barrel-chested with a shaven head but sporting thick sideburns, looked at her in a dumbfounded manner, as if she was an alien approaching a human being for the first time. He met her with an open smile that she didn't return with equanimity.

"You lost, sweetheart?" he asked.

"I'm looking for Paul Stevenson," she said. "I was told I'd find him here."

"Ain't nothing here but the best dancing girls and booze prices in the city!"

"I'm his sister. Is he here or not?"

The doorman, seemingly quite happy to accept that she was telling the truth, stepped aside, and gestured her into the building. She didn't look like trouble–she was too pretty.

"Go straight upstairs–office is first on the left."

Lucy nodded in acknowledgement and proceeded through the dim threshold. She climbed the stairs, noting the sex-show posters on the walls. They weren't sleazy; they didn't show intimate genitalia or full-on intercourse, but there were one or two posters with models holding onto polished poles or grasping glass dildos (other pictured models suggested they had theirs inserted, judging from the exhaustive, bitten-lip look on their faces). The white and pink text on many of the posters boasted of the club's V.I.P. facilities and star-studded corporate entertainment packages. If Paul really oversaw this place, he had only not fallen far from the tree but had rolled downhill after his descent, too.

She found the office door on the left as the barman had told her. Politely, she knocked a couple of times in succession. Since it was so quiet on the floor she was on, she could hear noises coming from inside the office clear as day. It immediately sounded hurried; calamitous.

Before Lucy knocked again, the door opened and out stepped a petite, black-haired beauty. She had on fishnet tights and a low-cut top. Suddenly, Lucy remembered her late teens, and how comparably she dressed then to what this girl was wearing. She rushed head-down past Lucy, pulling her miniskirt down, lest she flagrantly reveal to the conservative-looking woman what she had been feeding the proprietor.

Lucy slowly stepped into Paul's office. He sat in his chair behind his desk, and he was finishing buckling his belt. When the two of them saw one another neither wanted to break the silence. Lucy had to.

"Paul," she said, an acknowledgement, really. She recognised him–there was no denying it was her brother. His face (only now fuller); his brown hair (only now thinner); mere parts of the puzzle that made up who he now was.

"Lucy…" Paul said, resting his hands on the desk. "How did

you get here?"

Lucy closed the office door. It suddenly got darker in there; she saw the blinds that were hanging over the window and considered asking Paul to raise them higher to let in more sunlight.

"I drove. I had to find you, Paul. As in, well, *had* you found."

"*Had* me found? What do you mean?"

"You just disappeared! We had no idea where you were. Dad and I…" She left the rest of her sentence unexpressed. …*thought you were dead.*

"You had me tracked down?"

"By a professional, Paul. Someone who knew exactly where you'd gone–"

"–that's a bit over-the-top, Luce," he chastised her.

"Was it? We needed to know if you were still alive!"

Paul chuckled and began sifting through a pile of paperwork on the desk. Lucy didn't think he was looking for anything in particular– he was just nervous and was fiddling with things within reach.

"Of course, I'm still alive," he snapped. "Takes a lot to keep me down, Luce. Anyway, have a seat if you like."

Lucy sat down on a chair parallel to Paul. Each watched the other carefully for some moments.

"So," he said, initiating the small talk, "the big BBC let you have a day off?"

"Not really. I've been working mad hours since I started, even this morning. I start a lot earlier than you'd think."

Paul tapped his fingers on the desk. He was fidgety.

"Why are you here, Lucy? What do you want?"

"I came to see you," she leaned forward to urge him. "We miss you–*I* miss you, Paul! You left home after mum died–"

"–I *know* when mum died–"

"–but you didn't even stay after her funeral. She was barely in the ground when you drove off. You didn't even say goodbye properly."

Paul was softly biting on his lower lip, contemplating what to say next.

"I said goodbye to dad,' he responded. 'It's not my fault if he chose to ignore me afterward."

Lucy felt herself quivering as anger began to rise in her.

"What do you mean?"

Paul rocked back in his seat.

"Come on, Lucy–you were always their favourite! From when you did all the sports or the good jobs that you worked that helped them with the bills. They never had time for me after you left. I couldn't help out the way that you used to."

"Of course, they had time for you."

"Well, that's a matter of perspective, isn't it? Remember, I wasn't the one to leave for months on end while on courses for a big corporation."

"My job?" She was aghast. "Is that what this is about? Because I always put the family first. You, especially. I used to buy you anything you wanted."

"*You* put the family first? Did you really, Luce?"

There was no restraint in him now–the agony of his words stung her as if he'd been a wasp out to deliberately harm. She knew what he meant. It's what they all mean when they say something like that. But she didn't want to accuse him of being jealous or vindictive.

"Mum died, and you left dad on his own."

"You did, too, Luce," Paul said. "But if you want to be like that, *we both* left him."

Tears had started forming in Lucy's eyes, but were not strong enough yet for her to cry.

"Don't cry," he told her, passing her out a box of tissues from inside one of the desk drawers.

She whipped one out and dabbed her eyes.

"I tried… *really* hard," she said, maintaining composure. "You were young, Paul. But I had to get out, do what I wanted to do. I wanted to come back and help you, but when that right job offer came along, I knew it was what was best for me."

Paul's mobile phone began to ring. He plucked it out of his breast pocket, checked the caller I.D., and tapped the screen button to accept.

"What's up, Rudy?" He paused for the reply. "Okay, I'll be down soon. Take care of it for me. Thanks."

Paul placed the phone back into his pocket.

"Sorry, the floor staff is having trouble with a customer who has previous with his wandering hands."

Lucy pocketed the tissue. She was feeling better since Paul took the phone call. It gave them a chance to put the brakes on their rift.

"I suppose you want to know how I ended up here?" Paul queried.

Lucy looked around. The posters in here were like the ones that she saw on the way in. There wasn't much else besides the usual office equipment. Nothing against the law or out of the ordinary.

"It's your business," she replied, coolly.

"But I bet it makes a good weather girl like you look down on me?"

"I didn't say that. That's not fair."

"But looking in from outside, the difference is striking, right? I mean, you went off to have the six-figure salary and be on the TV every day–what did I do? What did *Paul* do? I'll tell you: he stayed behind, the pathetic son from a loveless marriage."

"I don't see what this has to do with anything, Paul."

"Come off it, Lucy," Paul chided. He seemed determined to haze on her untimely visit. "You were always the better child. After you left, I was like a shadow in that house. Mum's illness got worse. Dad started going out more, leaving me to look after the house *and* see to mum. Did you know that she once fell down the stairs?"

Lucy shook her head.

"She fell down the stairs, luckily only twisting her ankle. Where was dad? Out walking some bitch's mutt. We were both crying, and I picked mum up off the floor and carried her to the couch and she was so heavy–I was TEN YEARS OLD!"

Lucy didn't appreciate his raised voice, but she recognised that it was the young boy inside him who was yelling.

"I didn't know," Lucy said. "Nobody told me."

"I bandaged her up with help from the doctor–not the family one, the locum–and made sure she was stocked up on pills for her pain. And do you know what happened? One day, she was so out of it on the codeine that she thanked me for everything I'd been doing for her."

"What was wrong with that?"

"She thought I was *you*, Luce! She pulled me down so she could say in that soft-spoken voice of hers, *"Thank you, Lucy. Thank you for everything!"*. When she died, I knew it was no use staying there any longer. I got a job bartending here, then moved on to scouting for dancers–the rest is history. Once you get on the first rung of the ladder, the only way's up."

Lucy didn't know what to say to him. She genuinely hadn't known about the incident Paul had just relayed to her. She agreed that it was lucky for her mother that Paul had been there to pick her up and nurse her back to some form of good health. As for his career choice, it was out of her hands.

"So, what do we do now? I think we're done playing happy families," he bitterly remarked.

Lucy was sitting upright, her hands folded on her lap, in a pose that gave the impression she was in anticipation of news, good or bad. She recalled standing on the glass scales in her bathroom, waiting for the numbers. It felt like that.

"I don't know what I came here to expect, Paul. We've been apart for so long that… I was just happy I had found you. You aren't on social media; you're unlisted in the phonebook. The fee was worth it–it was a lot to find out where you were. But it was never about money or careers–it's about us and what we've got left."

Paul swivelled in his chair to face the window that was behind him. He pulled on the cord and raised the blinds halfway. The sunshine lay in horizontal strips across his desk. The room looked less sharp with natural light.

"Today's not a good day, Luce,' he said, still with his back to her. 'I've got a lot of work to do–no doubt you do too, right?"

He spun around then to face her, though not directly in her eyes. She knew he was investing in some false courage to hide his true feelings. They always did–those without the nerve to say what was really on their minds. Their eyes skittered this way and that, never straight, never locking on to their target. She didn't mind people who were truly minus of any mettle with which they could prop up their arguments, but the way Paul was acting now was selfish and impudent.

"Go home, Lucy," he said, speaking her name formally. "You found me, but I don't think it's where you hoped I'd be. I'm sorry if I disappointed you."

Her tears returned as she stood up.

"I was never disappointed, Paul. No matter what happens,

you're still my brother. You will *always* be that to me, whatever either of us do in life. I don't understand why you're being like this with me, but I'll go. Do you have anything you want to say to me before I leave?"

She saw Paul's head lowering as if in consideration at her request, hoping he would return with something to heal their wound and patch things up. He may have been hurting and summoning this last ounce of faux courage was empowering him to speak falsely.

"You're showing too much skin on TV."

Lucy heel-spun and opened the door to leave. A voluptuous blonde tottered past her in towering Perspex heels outside the office. She had a sympathetic look on her face as she caught sight of Lucy's dismay.

"What happened, honey? He break your heart? Never mind. Why don't you go home, put on a few pounds, and try again in a month or so? Take it from me: *the boys don't like to chew on bones.*"

Lucy was caught between sobs and laughter at the stripper's uniquely-uplifting words; words that might have only come out of a fallen angel's divine mouth.

***

In his office, Paul Stevenson is looking out of his window. He spies his big sister walking through the busy streets, distressed in her demeanour but keeping it to herself. She was never the kind to make a scene or cause a fuss. He's distraught at how their first meeting in years has turned out, but he's not surprised. It's the way he is now.

Hurting, he looks up at the sky through the window as his sister walks out of view. He doesn't know whether he'll see her again. He'd like to, but he's not the same brother she remembers. Life is different for each of them now. In the sky, there's not a pterodactyl in sight but the thunderous-looking clouds are gathering to cross a divide that separates siblings in love and in life. A divide that can't take the time to heal because it doesn't know how long the conflict will last, or if it will ever end at all. There can be no resolution until hearts and minds have reconciled, if that is ever to be an option–for them; for everyone.

Paul Stevenson recognises the clouds and knows it will rain. He hates the rain. He thinks he will catch the weather report on TV.

THE TENT

There was already damage in Bethany Childs' mind long before her attack ever took place; an area occupied by corruption which, even in her supernatural state, had refused to go away. Memories would be recycled until it was time for a reboot that would send the grimmest contents to the very front.

Before her fate exposed itself in the most dreadful and undignified of ways, snippets of her future had been evident throughout her childhood. Watching a late-night horror show; skimming over a TV sex ad; and the slaying of a neighbour's cat by a maniacal dog, were all puzzles in a jigsaw that had mapped out Bethany's young life. Had she been more aware of the enigmatic clues thrown up at her in her pubescence, Bethany might have heeded their warnings.

But Bethany had had her revenge on those who wronged her. Perhaps in the eyes of God and the Devil, their punishment was justified. Merciless, but retributed accordingly. This was no place to recount their horror or their crime.

It had been the tent. It was one of the earliest signs, that ghastly, triangular tabernacle sitting undisturbed in the sweeping country fields, which heralded her doom. It is here our story begins.

2

The trip to Aunt Jennifer's had been Bethany's second of that tense summer, the first having been to rescue the woman from her abusive husband, Uncle Mick. Bethany's dad–Aunt Jennifer's older brother–had given him a lesson in bare-knuckle boxing that day that Bethany was sure Uncle Mick would never forget. The young girl had witnessed her father beating the alcoholic with such ferocity that the image of the pulped, bloodied, bruised face of Uncle Mick had never left her, even in dreams.

Dad drove quietly with the sun visor down, while her mother

sat to his left cradling a basket of home-baked foods: gifts for Aunt Jennifer. Her parents were a happy couple, Bethany noted; an argument rarely came between them. Married as high-school sweethearts with one beautiful child. Other than the family disturbance that was Uncle Mick, life was generally sound to them.

"Are you going to play with Stephen?" mum asked, looking over her shoulder.

Bethany took notice. She had been watching the blue sky above the swaying green and yellow fields. A colourful mix, like something she had painted in her art class.

"Of course," she replied. "We get on well, don't we?"

"I know you do," mum spoke again, "only he's had it a bit rough lately, with his dad having been away for a bit and Aunt Jennifer taking unwell. If there's anyone who could cheer that boy up, it's you, Bethie."

Bethie! She despised that abbreviation of her beautiful name. But the woman who had blessed her with it retained more right than anyone to shorten it, stylise it how she wished, and Bethany could not argue.

They were soon approaching the end of the journey, turning onto a gravel path that was just wide enough to accommodate their car. Dad muttered that even a moped would have difficulty travelling this path, and mum just smiled. Tall trees hemmed each side of the road, and their wavering branches scratched at the roof of the car. Bethany could hear the branches tapping and scraping, while twigs swatted the windows. It was a rutted, narrow road, as if created only for those who preferred to travel precariously. Such roads were common in places like this, and it made any driver more cautious for fear of hitting anyone who might be taking a stroll.

The house came into view like a slide in a picture viewer. Aunt Jennifer had been left the picturesque four-bedroom home by their grandmother, who had thought the poor woman needed the security more than her son (who hadn't married anyone as violent and indignant as Uncle Mick). The old woman had been right in that sense, but Bethany's dad was certain that Mick was only married to Jennifer for the sole reason of acquiring the property if and when his sister finally succumbed entirely to her husband.

The sound of the tyres catching the gravel broke the silence, sending perhaps every bird in every tree skyward. The day remained calm otherwise, and not a hint of cold was in the air.

"Bethany, can you grab the bags from the back seat?"

The young girl nodded and pulled free the bags that had been belted down. Closing the car door, Bethany walked to the front of the house where her cousin Stephen came out to greet them.

"Aunt Linda! Uncle John!" the boy called, genuinely excited. He ran to his approaching relatives and gave each a tight hug. "And you, Bee!"

Another abbreviation, this one comical. She didn't mind; the boy was a year younger and not particularly bright for his age, but Bethany knew that his home life was often strained so she laid down the bags and squeezed him hard to let him know she was in good spirits, too.

"Little cousin!" she remarked. "Still ugly, like always!"

They laughed just as Aunt Jennifer appeared at the doorway. Bethany's dad was the first to notice how unsightly she looked–whatever illness had taken hold was slowly and duly working its way through her. An illness associated with an unhappy marriage.

"Hello, John; Linda," she called, smiling at them. "It's so nice to see you all."

The frail woman stepped out of the house and threw her arms around her older brother; Bethany's dad, John, could feel the bones in his sister's back; *Look how thin she's getting*, he thought, scaring himself at the unsettling revelation.

The reunion was cut short by a smashing sound from inside the house. Aunt Jennifer jumped in her brother's arms, as if it had happened right next to her.

"That'll be Uncle Mick," she said hastily. "He's redecorating! He's upstairs–we'll leave him to it. Come, let's get you all inside."

The five of them left the warmth of the sunlight and slipped into the house that felt like time forgot.

3

Bethany and Stephen sat in the living room drawing pictures with crayons as the adults prepared dinner in the kitchen. The kitchen was at the end of a long hallway; the house reminded

Bethany of something out of Victorian times or like in one of those American prairie TV shows, where a busload of children grew up in a brooding hulk of a building only recently introduced to electricity. There was a cultural feel to the place that Bethany associated with her late grandmother; nothing that alluded to usual perceptions that the homes of the elderly should be dim, floral-scented tragedies, but instead something that promoted warmth and brimmed with life and experience.

She could hear the adults talking, but ever so quietly, almost unperceptively; and above, Uncle Mick, methodically pacing around on the first floor, as he pasted and painted and papered the walls. Once or twice Bethany thought she heard a swear word or two rolling down the stairs; the insalubrious colour of Uncle Mick's language.

"Well?" Stephen asked, detaching her from her thoughts. "What have you drawn?"

"Um," she started, fumbling around on the floor at the spread of paper. "I sketched this: it's a fashion piece. Here we've got the head-dress and the robe, with the gold and–what?"

The young boy simply stared. He was unimpressed. The raised eyebrow told her so.

"You drew something better?" she asked, a little pointedly.

Stephen nodded.

"It's something that's real. I've seen it."

Bethany was intrigued–she held out her hand and he passed the paper over to her. Turning it the right way around, she recognised the playful attempt at blue sky, and the yellow sticks of corn or wheat or whatever it was that grew in the fields around the place. It was the form at the centre of the A4 sheet that held her attention: a green tent, unmistakable in its triangular shape. There was something immensely striking about its composition; although lacking any degree of photo realism or representation she was still certain that it was a tent. *A real wannabe Picasso!* she mused.

"It looks like a tent," Bethany said. "Just an ordinary green tent."

Stephen snatched the paper back.

"It's not ordinary! It's haunted."

"Haunted? How do you know?"

There was a look in the boy's eyes, something that indicated his statement was down to frightful suspicion and not acquired from any

115

hard evidence, collected, and/or examined.

"I've been to see it with my friends, Kenny and Danny," Stephen explained. "We went there just two weeks ago. It was shut but Kenny said he had been there the day before and the door was open!"

Bethany wasn't impressed.

"So? Maybe some homeless person lives in it? Or someone camping. Doesn't mean it's haunted! That's just childish."

"I'm telling you, that tent is real, and it's spooky."

"Have you seen inside it?" she asked

"No, because it's haunted. There might be something evil living inside."

Just then, Aunt Jennifer made an appearance; and in some uncanny spousal synchronicity, Uncle Mick also appeared. But it was only Aunt Jennifer who stepped into the living room to be with the children.

"Are you alright, kids?" she asked them. "Dinner's almost ready."

"Thank God," Mick muttered. His face and hands were splattered with paint. "I've been up there all morning on my own. Whoever invented the bloody idea needs their head kicked!"

Aunt Jennifer did her best to maintain the kids' attention and directed away from the paint-splattered brute.

"Bethany, how is school? Your mum and dad said that you're doing well in art."

Bethany nodded to confirm.

"I like to draw, and so does my friend, Michelle. We do projects together that we often get certificates for."

Uncle Mick walked across the room, muttering, "At least one child in this family has its head screwed on."

"Well, good for you, darling," Aunt Jennifer praised. "Is that your picture?" She was referring to the fashion piece. "Wow! Maybe one day you'll be designing clothes for the stars!"

Stephen raised his tent drawing.

"I drew this, mum."

Aunt Jennifer took the paper from him. She looked at it disapprovingly.

"That's not the old horrible thing by the railway bridge, is it,

Stephen? You stay away from that… that *tent*. It's dirty, and nobody knows what's inside. Could be anything. Or anyone. Just stay away– do you understand?"

She returned his Picasso-in-practise and made to return to the kitchen.

"Dinner will be in ten minutes. Make sure your hands are washed, and then come through to the kitchen. We'll be sitting out in the back garden to enjoy the day."

As she left, she coughed so hard that it was as if something malicious had settled in her lungs and was refusing to let go.

4

The day out back was enjoyable, for their hard work preparing dinner was rewarded by a spot of sunshine that shone directly onto them. Even the winged insects stayed away long enough for them to eat and clear their meal, although the prying eyes of an interested squirrel or two hadn't escaped them. Aunt Jennifer sat with her brother and his wife at one side of the long wooden rectangular table; but Uncle Mick dined inside, chewing on his meal with apparent resentment as he stared at the group outside the window. Bethany's dad knew that their appearance today was likely to have fuelled any rage in Mick, but if the brute wanted to stir up any kind of trouble– verbal or physical–he would soon set him right.

"Eat up all of your bread," Aunt Jennifer urged her son. "It's good for you. Your Aunt Linda baked it herself."

The boy looked at both women, unaware just how much each wanted the world for their children. The design of a child, an implication of innocence.

"I will," he told them. "With this ham the bread tastes amazing!"

Bethany gulped down her lemonade. She was enjoying her food too and was really immersing herself in the environment in which her cousin lived. She thought how commonplace it was where she lived: there were nosey dogs instead of curious squirrels; gas-belching cars in place of carbon dioxide-drunk trees–even the cat-collecting old crone who lived across her street seemed grumpier than Uncle Mick.

The delight of having her family visit was evident in Aunt Jennifer's eyes and in her smile; in every gesture the frail woman could display. Bethany sussed that there was nothing else in the world that the lady would prefer doing on a warm day like this than be surrounded by the people who truly loved and cared for her. It was healthy for her–for Stephen too–to be reminded that, while they resided like hermits, they were still very much a solid part of the family.

Stephen led Bethany to the swing that Uncle Mick had set up at the bottom of the garden. It was a rusting blue frame, but the ropes held taut and the seat was level and stable enough to hold either of them. Bethany sat on it first while Stephen pushed her gently.

"Have you given it any thought?" he asked from behind.

"About what?"

"The tent," he continued. "The haunted one."

"No, actually, I haven't. Why? You heard what your mum said, that you were to stay away from it."

Stephen pushed.

"I'm just saying, maybe we could investigate it–see what it's like inside."

Bethany scraped her shoes on the dirt beneath the seat to slow herself. She held onto the ropes as she turned to face him.

"Are you serious?"

Stephen nodded slowly, a grin forming more gradually.

"But what if we get caught? I mean, how far is the tent from here?"

A hopeful expression flitted across his young, chubby face.

"It's only about twenty or so minutes' away. It's beyond the back woods, past the trees where the old railway bridge is. We wouldn't be gone long, so we wouldn't really be far from here."

Bethany chewed over the idea. She had to acknowledge some curiosity over the mysterious tent, but the possible dangers that may be lying in wait quelled that craving for knowledge. What if someone occupied it? Who would they be? And why was it there in the first place? All those questions suddenly increased the desire to know–a psychology that provided sustenance for a child's hunger to explore.

"I overheard dad saying to my mum that we should stay the night," Bethany told him. "I think he's worried about your mum.

He wants to keep an eye on her. Do you think..."

"What? That we should go tonight?" Stephen exclaimed.

"As long as we don't get too close, I think we could manage a little trip. What do you say?"

Grinning again, he began to push his big cousin.

<u>5</u>

By the time evening arrived the family had retreated into the house where, surprisingly, Uncle Mick had set a roaring fire in the living room. He didn't receive any thanks from his in-laws except for a hug from his wife who remarked on the homely, warm feel of the room. He basked in her gratefulness before disappearing upstairs.

There was a radio on the cabinet in the living room which Aunt Jennifer suggested that they listen to. She switched it on and tweaked the dial until she found some soft music playing. There were no objections to her choice.

The adults sat on the couch while the two youngsters prepared themselves for bed. The time was going on 8pm and weariness had settled upon the party, but Bethany and Stephen were hiding their energies.

"We're going upstairs now," said Stephen, approaching his mum. "I'll get the fold-out bed and make it up for Bee, okay? Good night, mum. Goodnight, Aunt Linda, Uncle John."

Aunt Jennifer kissed her son and thanked him. Bethany announced that she would help him make the bed. The children bade goodnight to their respective parents and together they walked up the stairs to Stephen's room, the twinkle in their eyes sparkling like jewels at the thought of their forthcoming adventure.

***

The remainder of the evening was uneventful, and all four adults were sound asleep by 11pm. Uncle Mick was snoring soundly in his bed with his wife, while Bethany's parents slept on a futon downstairs.

The moonlight acted as a torchlight, thus enabling Bethany and Stephen to exit the bedroom without incident. They had redressed with each adding a jacket to their earlier attire, and, with one behind the other, Bethany led the youngster quietly down the hallway to the top of the stairs. Their subsequent descent was flawless in its silent precision.

Tip-toeing through the living room, Stephen brushed past Bethany and opened a kitchen drawer.

"We'll need the back-door key," he whispered, carefully feeling around in the drawer with his hand. "To lock it outside, and then for when we get back."

Stephen closed the drawer softly and momentarily held up the key in triumph. He inserted it into the lock, turned it, and gently, with a devilish cunning opened the door just enough for them to squeeze through, before locking it again on the outside.

"Okay?" asked Bethany. "Lead the way."

They started off down the back garden–where again the moonlight acted as their guide–running now, past the large table, beyond the swings, and into the shadows of the bushes. They had woods the length of two football fields to cover, with a time-length that Stephen had estimated to be around twenty minutes. They would manoeuvre their way through the woods, traverse the cornfields, and then cross the disused railway bridge to the location of the tent. They soon found that negotiating fallen branches and muddy puddles wasn't easy in the dark. The moon was now glitter-balling its light through the tree canopy, bending and curving the bough-strewn duff and skewering their perspective of the land ahead.

They eventually reached the woodland's edge, a victory akin to a try or a touch-down back in the real world. Bethany thanked her younger cousin sarcastically for the excursion, as she itched herself from the ankles up. She was certain she had been bitten en masse by flying, nocturnal insects.

Stephen tried to perk her up.

"There's not far to go now, Bee," he assured her. "Once we make it through these cornfields, it's just the bridge to cross and then we're there."

Bethany sighed, accepting that it was she who planted the seeds of their trek anyway, and hurried him on. They had already been stumbling nearly fifteen minutes by the time they exited the woods. At least the cornfields were only, at worst, waist-high.

The first stalk whacked against her side and she fumed.

"How are you not getting hurt in this?" she said aloud, almost growling at him.

Stephen glanced back.

"Because I've done this before."

Bethany angrily swiped another stalk away. The bristling of swaying stalks sounded like a hundred brush-heads rubbing against one another around her. Their light was brighter now, the moon giving the fields a patina of silvery-gold shine and making everything around them much easier to see.

She stomped and kicked, flattened, and snapped much of the remaining way, while Stephen's lighter, more fleeting, body could breeze through. She could see his small frame ahead, pushing through the stalks with ease, darting this way and that; and she was also aware of a creeping unease, something unsettling that was trying to consume them in this night maze. As if they were being watched from afar by eyes that could see everything. No, it was as if it was *she* that was being observed.

The rusting frame of the bridge appeared seconds after they both slipped out of the cornfields.

Stephen stood silently, his hands on his hips, resting. Bethany caught up and stood beside him.

"Remind me never to eat corn flakes again!"

Her light-hearted remark made the boy smile.

"We're about two minutes from the tent," he calmly informed her. "Can you feel it?"

Bethany shuddered. Quite suddenly the air became cooler, and the wind was picking up around them and whistling through the fields behind.

"Feel what?"

"Like there's something here," Stephen said, staring into the distance. "Watching us."

"Your mind's playing tricks on you! There's nothing to be afraid of. C'mon, we'd better hurry. We've spent too much time out here already."

They started to march, this time on much smoother ground. The ground beneath them was dark-coloured and beat, but kind to their soles.

Stephen squatted, urging Bethany to do the same.

"What is it?" she whispered.

"Nothing. I just wanted to make sure that if there was someone there, we'd be out of their sight. When we go down over that ridge, the tent's in full view."

They duck-walked a couple of yards before sliding to the edge of the grassy ridge, their chins resting on the grass.

"Look over to the right," instructed Stephen. "You can't miss it."

Bethany brushed her hair from her face. The wind was starting to get annoying, but she had to see clearly. She shuffled forward and, like a meerkat, raised her head to peer over the ridge. Sure enough, down to the right, was the tent.

Unlike in the boy's crude drawing she had viewed earlier that day, here was the thing stark against the backdrop of a thick sky. Its dense and distinct form–pegged to the ground–never moved despite the wind blowing into it. It was like a solid prism encroaching into her frame of view.

"Does it look empty?" Bethany started, suddenly remembering Stephen by her side.

"It's hard to tell. Now, if someone is inside, they could be sleeping."

Stephen thought for a moment.

"What do we do?"

"We've seen it now, I believe you," she conceded. "I don't think we need to get any closer."

"But maybe we could check it a little, even just stay out here," he suggested.

Bethany remained staring at the tent. She couldn't tell if the front was closed or not.

"But I believe you that the tent's real," she said. "You win, okay?"

A sudden gust blew over them, and for the first time, Bethany saw the entrance flap open.

"It's not zipped down! It's not!" said Stephen, excitedly. If it wasn't for him lying down, he might've been jumping in the air.

"That does not mean we need to go in," Bethany told him.

"I'll go," Stephen said. "Just a bit, enough to see inside when the wind next blows. If there's anyone there, we're off. Okay?"

Bethany rolled her eyes.

"This could be dangerous," she said, the tone of her voice bordering on worry. "It could be someone who's a right crackpot, and then what do we do? Race through the fields like the Children of the Corn? No, thanks, Stephen *King*; we need to get home!"

He didn't listen to her; before she knew it, he was half standing and was about to approach the tent. She tried pulling him back, but her fingers slipped from his jacket.

"See you down there, Bee!"

Stephen crouched and made his way to the clearing where the tent was pitched. He kept to the one side, and, with the aid of some tall, prickly grass, remained unseen. Bethany watched him move like a character in a computer war game, with all the machismo and bravado of every ten-year old boy she had ever known.

Within a minute, he was close to the front of the tent. The two of them kept their eyes fixed on it should any occupants decide to vacate it for a midnight toilet break, or whatever. Bethany supposed that since they had come all this way it would be a waste to go back with nothing learnt. Besides, maybe a quick glance into this marquee-home would put an end to the mystery. Yeah, that was it: she would get closer.

By the time Bethany made it to the tent, Stephen was already peeking in. The wind had blown the entrance open again and he saw that there was no body–shape, figure, or otherwise–in there. The thought hadn't occurred to them that as they had been spying on the tent, someone may have been spying on them.

"I can see stuff," said Stephen, holding the entrance flap open. "But there's definitely no-one in there."

Bethany crept closer.

"Doesn't look haunted, either. I think we can say that there's nothing to worry about here."

She felt an urge to move further in, to explore the innards of the tent. She could just make out papers and bottles, and something ragged that looked like a well-used sleeping bag. The silent night enveloped them; encouraging her too, to go in.

On her hands and knees, she slowly crawled forward. Her hands could feel the cold nylon of the groundsheet, and the prickly grass beneath. There were crumbs that pressed into her palms, which she wiped off hurriedly. Stephen remained on the outside, holding the flap open, keeping watch.

She felt the rubber handle of a small torch and after some probing, the switch. She looked back at Stephen, holding up the torch to show him. He looked in, nodding in acknowledgement.

She switched it on, and the inside of the tent lit up. In later years, Bethany would remember this moment as perhaps the main catalyst that disturbed and broke her mind; the one event that awoke the demon creature, Amy, alerting her of Bethany's plight. Had she not switched on the torch; the sordid remnants of an addict's haven would have remained unseen.

Pornography magazines appeared to be the favoured leisure pursuit here; Bethany unwittingly shone the circle of light over the glossy spreads of naked women of bygone eras; women with their breasts hanging out, holding and displaying them wantonly for the viewer's pleasure. She gasped at the 'mystery' she had solved; at the gross treasure she had found. There were pictures of stocking-legged women exhibiting themselves alone; some with one or multiple male partners; others cavorting with women with tongues and fingers and various sex toys. In other magazines nearby there was more of the same, except one or two spreads featured women experimenting with all kinds of phallic objects.

The young girl felt sick to her stomach. She wanted to cry out, alert Stephen, but she could not let him see this filth. She dropped the torch and the light gleamed upon bottles of assorted colours and substances, some without labels but all recognisable as containers of beer. She doubted whether it was beer inside them, judging from the acrid smell they gave off.

She fumbled for the torch, close to tears and vomiting. She wished she hadn't turned the damn thing on. Gripping it she thumbed the switch back and killed the light. In the darkness, she could still see those glossy, naked parts, hanging and spreading–things being inserted.

She crouched past Stephen as she exited; he let go of the flap and watched her as she stood, shaking uncontrollably.

"You okay, Bethany? What was in there? What did you see?"

With much effort, Bethany tried to compose herself.

"Nothing. It was nothing, Stephen. Come, we need to go. We've been out long enough."

Stephen slowly got to his feet.

"You sure you're okay?"

Bethany grabbed hold of his hand.

"Stephen, never, ever come near this... *thing* again. Promise me that?"

The young boy simply looked on, perplexed and speechless.

"PROMISE ME!"

He buckled a bit as she reached out for his hand.

"Sure, Bee. Okay. Please, let go–you're hurting my hand! Hey, why are you crying?"

"From now on, you've no further business being here. *Listen to your mother.*"

She dragged him away and back onto the tracks that would return them back to the cornfields. They didn't speak a single word all the way home, but each knew there were a thousand things to say.

<u>6</u>

The next morning, after a vivid, horrendous succession of nightmares, Bethany tried to forget about the tent. She was still a young girl, still sensitive to the world, to balking at pharmaceuticals being tested on animals and to livestock being slaughtered for the convenience of fast food. She hadn't allowed herself to grow up but last night she had walked into something diabolical, something not fit for her. She saw magazine images of the boundaries of human contentment, though not wholly representative of; looked at consented degradation and glossy snapshots of acts that schools taught were only fit for love. It disturbed her, shook her inside, but what else did she expect to find? Was there a rainbow ending in the tent? Had she hoped it would lead to wherever had Alice went? It was a discovery that would now remain with her forever.

In the next few months, as more and more warnings of her impending doom were spelled out to her in various devilish-inspired ways, she would find out from Stephen that the tent was no longer there. The land on which it stood had been farmed and conjoined to the nearby cornfields. It was considered a waste of resource, otherwise.

In dreams for the next few years, up until her fifteenth birthday, she would sometimes see that swamp-green prism in the field; and behind her a train would speed by, and as it rolled along the tracks–across the bridge–its squeaks and rattles and hoots would mock her. She would dream that she was standing beside the tent, and the canvas entrance would be flapping in the wind, catcalling her to enter.

And in Hell, a creature would be sitting waiting patiently to begin the young girl's retribution.

THE VOICE IN THE BUSH

1

For the best part of that Saturday morning, Sam's parents had argued and thrown things at each other. This was an act that was becoming second nature at weekends. It was no longer shocking for Sam to hear the familiar sound of a mug shattering off the living room linoleum, or a TV remote against a wall.

Sam often thanked God that they had no neighbours. At least, none in the immediate proximity of their rented cottage. An elderly couple lived down the road and they had the biggest tree in their garden Sam had ever seen. Their big house stood like a brick sentry at the bottom of the road that seemed like forever away. Sam had climbed that tree a few times, usually when she knew the Wilsons were out. Mrs. Wilson had caught her once scaling the thick trunk like a hurried cat; and when the girl descended the old woman explained to her that one of the things more harrowing than tidying a few snapped branches was having to collect a small body from the base and explain to her parents why their child's back had broken. Sam had overheard in one conversation between her parents and the Wilsons that the Wilsons had lost two of their adult children in the last decade, and it was a bereavement each couple said they wouldn't wish on anybody.

A song with beachy vibes waved out of the radio in the kitchen of Sam's home; a tune that was brooding and melancholy. She sat on her bed, bouncing a tennis ball from a triple-pack she had bought from the local newsagent. She had saved some of her dinner money from school that week to build a little nest-egg for the weekend. The tennis ball had that faint sward-rubber scent that most–if not all–new tennis balls have. A summerly fragrance that left a gratifying, mental imprint. The soft fuzz in her hands felt nice and it meant she could grip the ball better. She was improving with her catching, having had so much practise over the spring and early summer days. Sam kept her bedroom door closed these weekend mornings, but her parents' arguments usually found a way through the walls.

About 12pm–around the time Sam had counted over one-hundred ball tosses as she lay back on her bed–her father knocked on her bedroom door and poked his head in. She sat up with the tennis ball in her hand, frozen at one-hundred and eleven.

"Dad?" she blurted.

Her father, face purple from exertion or temperament, spoke to her calmly but firmly, which to Sam, was usually a sign that her parents' differences were resolved–even if only temporarily. There was always Sunday.

"Come on, Samantha," he said. "We need to leave in the next five if we're going to make it to the football. Kick-off's at half past."

Excited, Sam tossed the ball onto her pillow and jumped off the bed.

"Just got to find my shoes, Dad," she told him, but by then he had already withdrawn from the opening.

With her head down with a purpose, she looked for her shoes.

2

They parked in the furthest away spot in the car park of the football ground's attached social club. Exiting, they walked side by side to the main gate; a lone figure sat smoking a cigarette inside a bricked recess that was the ticket booth. When the smoking-man saw them approach, he quickly extinguished his roll-up between his thumb and middle finger, and only accepted the admission price for her father.

"Kid's a future supporter," he said from within the smoke-scented alcove, his presumption noted.

Sam's dad thanked him for the gesture, took his ticket and ushered her in. It was an open ground, not a stadium. The pitch was lush-green, mown inch-perfect, and to Sam, it smelled like tennis balls.

A young afternoon sunshine warmed them as they walked by pockets of other supporters. Sam didn't take much of it in–not the opposition colours nor the huddled bodies discussing each team's earlier performances. It was all just noise to her. Noise with the odd interjected imprecation to bolster the speakers' sentiment.

She had heard some of that language before, at weekends.

They stopped at the terracing and found a spot on the concrete steps to sit. The sheltered enclosure was to their left and due to the bright sun, many supporters hid away in there, cool and cosy in the interior shade. Sam didn't mind where she was told to sit. The stepped terraces curved around the field; a design put in place to cater for the spectators during the summer games. There was also some scrubland at the farthest away part of the field. Sam could not see any trees as big as the Wilson's tree from where she was sitting. She was eager to get up and explore, just a little jaunt whilst the footballers played.

Two red dugout shelters that looked like enlarged, hollowed Monopoly hotels to Sam, faced them from the other side of the field. Beside her, her dad was counting some coins in his hands. The terraces were getting livelier. Sam didn't bother. She rarely had an issue with crowds. A few weeks before, she was picked for a school outing with a visiting member of the Royal family. Princess Anne, sole daughter of Queen Elizabeth II, had been invited to officiate the opening of a particularly important recycling eco-centre on the outskirts of Sam's town. It had been a massive visit that preceded with enormous arrangement; black-suited men with walkie-talkies killing it at being James Bond. Kings and Queens Sam only really knew from playing chess in school during their 'golden time'. Princesses were Disney's game.

Bang on time, the players ran out of the pavilion and onto the pitch: the home team splendid in maroon; the visiting team in a bright, sky blue. A tall, black and yellow referee followed carrying a football; he himself, tailed by similarly-dressed linesmen. They were like a trio of giant bumble-bees.

Both sets of supporters whistled and cheered their team on, each side looking to fire up their sportsmen, many just young men whose fathers were friends with the local, rural support, or had at least grown up with them. Was this grassroots football? Sam didn't understand the word 'grassroots'. At her age, she processed it too literally, as children are wont to do. Whenever she heard of grassroots *anything*, she thought it meant digging up the ground to reveal the tender beginnings of the blades.

Her dad, finished from counting his money, looked down at her and said to follow him to the food stand. Excited at the prospect of filling her tummy with something like a hot dog or roll on sausage–either food item loaded with a dollop of tangy, tomato sauce–she jumped up eagerly from the step.

The queue had diminished; but the burly, moustachioed vendor behind the raised counter looked as busy as ever, shuffling from hot plate to hot plate, sink to sink. Those certificates stuck to the inside wall of his built-in kitchen well-earned. When he turned to see he had two new customers waiting, he cleaned his hands over a washbasin and went to the counter, drying his hands with some kitchen roll.

"What can I get you, pal?" he asked Sam's dad, tossing the crumpled paper into a bin.

"A mince pie and a tea, please," Sam's dad replied, before turning to his daughter: "And what about you, Samantha? Same as last time?"

She nodded.

"And a hot dog–oh, without onions–and a can of Coke. Zero."

The vendor turned and went about fulfilling their order. Sam's dad pointed out the table with the condiments to get her to take note. Sam walked over to it to survey the contents on offer: ketchup, brown sauce, mustard–all good, branded varieties. She didn't like mustard, felt it was too thick and spicy, but she would settle for a squiggle of ketchup atop the sausage.

The vendor handed over the goods whilst her dad pushed over a pile of pound coins on the counter. With this transaction processed they turned to go to the table for extras.

Sam almost bumped into the old smoking-man from the ticket booth.

"I'm sorry, my dear," he apologised to her, quickly seizing her by the shoulders as if to prevent knocking her over.

"I'm fine," Sam said, gripping her food.

"My sight nowadays!" the old man whined to her dad, feigning a sad look with a penitent tone of voice. "I'm almost blind!"

He went on: "Reminds me of an old saying: *The eye is the lamp of your body; when your eye is clear, your whole body also is full of light; but when it is bad, your body also is full of darkness".*"

130

"Wasn't that in a Dylan song?" Sam's dad asked whilst spooning sugar into his tea.

The old man shrugged.

"I don't know. Maybe. Let's just hope today's referee has eyes that work better than mine!"

The old man walked past them to go to the counter, where Sam noticed that the vendor was working in the back, unaware of his new customer. The old man turned to look back at Sam, and he gave her a wave and a wink. Sam saw that his hand was crooked, deformed (she couldn't remember it being like that at the ticket booth) and his eyes seemed darker, blacker, as if they could read into her mind. *No white,* she thought. *His eyes have no white in them.*

She became detached from this eerie moment by her dad shaking one of the sauce bottles in front of her face.

"Hey, do you want red sauce on the hot dog?"

When she regained her full concentration, Sam turned to face her father, uttering, "Uh? Oh, yes, please."

Her dad took the food from her small hands, which had been gripping the roll tight enough to leave indents through the napkin. She watched him squeeze the sauce out from the bottle, producing a red wavy line along the top of the hot meat.

Before he finished, and they returned to their seating on the terraces, Sam took one last look at the food stall. She couldn't see the burly vendor anywhere in there.

The old man had vanished, too.

<u>3</u>

Expletives aside, Sam was enjoying listening to the colourful banter bouncing verbally from the supporters around her. Even her dad joined in with the shouting, most of which was directed at the referee or nearby linesman.

The desire to explore the outer football ground started to gnaw at her whilst she sat and watched the men play. Sometimes, she thought she could smell cigarette smoke right beside her; though, from looking all around, nobody seemed to be smoking. A few bodies vaped but that was all. The image of the old man with the withered hand stayed with her.

The referee blew his whistle at once following a nasty challenge; both teams' supporters howled and booed at the tackle, quickly growling their disciplinary opinions.

"*JESUS CHRIST, REF!*" someone in the enclosure hollered.

"Show him the red card, referee!"

More angry shouting persisted, insisting that the ref get the "hacking bastard off the park". Bravely, the ref stuck to his guns, and Sam watched the referee issue a yellow card to the offending visiting player; all the while the home player lay on the ground foetal-like in obvious pain.

"Will that man be okay, Dad?" Sam asked.

Her dad, infuriated by the referee's decision to show the yellow card, cooled down after a few moments.

"He'll be fine after a sit-down and oranges at half-time."

The game resumed, but not before the young man who had been badly tackled spent some time being tended to by the physio. He eventually got back up; Sam heard someone say that he would be walking with a limp in future. But the player started running again and so Sam refused to believe in his foretold disability.

Five minutes before the whistle for half-time, Sam asked her dad if she could go and play in the surrounding field. He told her yes, but to be back by the end of the second half.

"Don't speak to anybody. And *don't* leave the area. Your mum would have a heart attack if you were to go missing again."

Sam promised her dad that she would not disappear out of his sight. She walked on behind the sheltered enclosure, an area the sun rejected this early in the afternoon. Laughter rang out from one of the enclosure's openings. As Sam passed the opening in the brickwork, she looked in and thought that in amongst the group of laughing men she saw the old man; he was still smoking, removing the cigarette with his wilted hand, and staring out *at her*, *deliberately*.

Shuddering, she continued walking past the enclosure, leading out onto the grass that abutted the edge of the terraces. When she strolled out of the shade, she re-entered the warm sunshine and picked up her pace.

The shrill sound of the referee's whistle from the football pitch sent a flurry of birds heading for the sky in the bushes around her.

She turned to see the players wearily walking off the pitch and head into the dressing rooms for "a sit-down and some oranges". Sam then realised just how far away she was from where her father was sitting; he was just a little figure in her sight, recognisable by the colour of his jacket.

She turned away and continued her trek. As she neared the bushes, she again sniffed that same cigarette smoke, but she could not see it at all. It was strong and distracting, like the smells permanently pitched outside the old pubs on the way home from school…

…and from when they entered the grounds by the ticket booth.

<u>4</u>

A small bird danced around inside the bush that Sam stood before. The bird flitted from branch to branch. It was a frenzied jig. Sam could not tell if it was trapped and freaking out, or if it genuinely was happy frittering around in there.

"Hey, little guy!" she spoke to it. She wanted to reach in, to see if she could clear a path with her arm and help set it free; although, it was quite fun and hypnotic to watch, and disturbing it might scare it off, she thought.

Only, she *did* want to set the little thing free, but then it stopped jumping and tweeting altogether. The rustling of the leaves as the bird had hopped frantically from one branch to the next, fluttering its wings, ceased instantly.

The football field was empty, save for two or three bib-wearing substitutes that had taken to one end of the park to warm up. Sam then turned her attention back to the bush, to the silence it was now exuding. Somewhere inside the shrub, inside its darkened innards, a tiny bird body dropped to the ground, now a lifeless, feathered vessel. Sam saw its sudden descent and, dishearteningly, heard with unblemished clarity the soft thump it made as it hit the ground.

Sam wanted again to reach in, to touch the thing just to see if it really had died. Perhaps it had just knocked itself out; in her computer games, it often happened: a character after a collision or a fight would stay motionless on the ground onscreen, respawning after a few minutes. However, no matter how intently she watched, there was no sign of the little bird reviving.

"Sad, isn't it?"

Sam, startled, turned around expecting to meet the source of the voice, but to her surprise found no-one there. It had come from in front. From the bush.

She looked all around the shrubbery in case there was someone hiding nearby. It had been the croaky-sounding voice of an older man, not so different from the vocals of that of the old, smoking-man, who re-entered her thoughts, unsettling her again.

"Is somebody in there?" she asked, a little foolishly. Surely there was not. She couldn't see–

"Do you mourn for the bird?"

"What?" Sam replied, continuing to search for the mouthpiece of the voice.

"I asked, is it upsetting you that it's dead?"

Sam thought more about the voice's question than consider the fact she was conversing with a talking bush.

"I think so," she replied, slowly. "But, doesn't everything have to die?"

The green bush was neither shielding nor shedding certainties of any bogeymen lurking in its form, Sam could justify. Of course, the idea of a talking bush only came from fiction, like something from a children's tale or that long-standing fable from the Bible.

"Not everything *has* to die," said that same old man's voice, in a distinctive tone.

Sam looked deeper into the bright, sunlit bush; she even pushed aside some of the leaves just in case there *was* a person in there, camouflaged like a soldier. That old man? Behind her, a round of clapping resounded from the terraces as both teams jogged back onto the football pitch.

"I'd better get back to my dad–he's back there, watching the game," Sam told the bush, or whomever was speaking out of it.

"Oh," said the voice from within the bush, "but, are you sure you don't want to stay and talk with me for a bit? There are things I need to share with you, *Samantha*. Important things."

Sam's curiosity speared her on.

"What kind of things? And, how do you know my name?"

"I know a lot about you, young lady! If you want to go, then go. If you'd rather stay here–at least until the game is over–I'm sure we could pass the time telling stories."

The bush trembled as if invisible hands were shaking it. A quick burst of laughter followed; again, *disembodied* glee.

"I want to know who *you* are."

The trembling stopped.

"Oh, really?" said the voice.

"Yes," said Sam. "Tell me your name. You know mine."

"Okay, that's fair enough. But you must keep it to yourself, Samantha: it's Dorian."

"That's a funny name!" Sam said, with a chuckle of her own.

"Yes, you might find that it is, but I'm known by many more; however, today you can call me 'Dorian'. Now, shall we begin with a story?"

Sam sat impatiently, awaiting whatever tales the thicket wished to tell.

<u>5</u>

Dying, it seemed, did not necessarily mean 'the end'. According to Dorian, anyway. He (Sam assumed it was a 'he' due to the grumbling masculinity in the voice) let Sam know an interesting fable or two about lions and old men—all with the denouement of reincarnation. It did strike her young mind as peculiar, that she was sharing this odd exchange with something in the bush she could not see, but the imaginative part of her overshadowed any real queries that may have been idling. To her eight-year old mind, she simply was conversing with an unseen human. For all she knew, a hidden radio could have been implanted deep in the bush, and someone was playing a joke. Weird and creepy, but a joke, nonetheless.

"So, do you understand what I'm saying to you?" asked Dorian, as if colourful tales of make-believe could have their moral messages decoded by prepubescent minds.

Sam didn't have to try hard to picture the dying lion; not unlike the patriarchal image of Disney's Mufasa, but collapsed outside its cave whilst enemies frittered 'round with their own dishonourable ideas of retaliation and revenge. It may have been easy enough to take in—the whole 'circle of life' thing—but it didn't make it seem any more comprehensible. Coming back from the dead?

"Kind of," Sam eventually answered, pulling at the grass she was kneeling on. "Like, it doesn't matter how we live or if people are good to us, we'll get the chance to come back and start again. Is that right?"

"*"And that from a child thou hast known the holy scriptures".*"

Sam regarded the bush puzzledly.

"What does that mean?"

"It means you're perceptive, Samantha. Gloriously-so. Which is why I wished to speak to you."

"This is too weird!" she exclaimed, finally. It was the first time she had genuinely considered doubting the scenario playing out before her.

"It's up to you if you want to believe in me," Dorian said, in an indifferent manner.

"I can't even see you! And bushes don't normally speak to people. Not in real life, anyway."

The bush shook with laughter.

"But this *is* real life, Samantha! You've been sleeping for some time; now, it's time to wake up!"

A branch struck out from the centre of the bush and poked her in the chest.

"*Oww!*" Sam cried. "What was *that* for?!"

"Did that feel real enough to you?"

She rubbed at the spot through her jacket where the tip of the branch had struck. It had quickly retracted into the bush.

"Just don't do that again!" Sam warned whilst manoeuvring backwards, cautious of another attack.

"I'm sorry," Dorian apologised. "You had to know that I am real. Tell you what; before you leave here today, I will demonstrate what I mean on the field behind you."

Sam turned 'round, only to see the football players playing as normal.

"You're not going to hurt any of them, are you?"

"Not directly, Samantha, though, it is someone's time to go."

When she turned back, she could have sworn that there were two red orbs staring out at her from inside the bush.

The cigarette smoke had also returned.

6

Dorian let Samantha know when it was time. There were no inspiring parting words, no more Bible quotes to take heart from; in fact, the voice barely revealed anything until it was almost all over on the field.

"I want you to do something for me, Samantha."

Sam regarded the bush with sudden interest and worry.

"What?"

"I want you to pick a number. Between... one and twenty-five."

Sam thought it over. "Hmm... seventeen."

"Too bad, they've already retired that one. Try again."

It wasn't that easy for her to do, despite how simple the question seemed, for she didn't know why a particular number was of importance to Dorian. She felt obliged to answer correctly; she did not want to keep choosing any that had been 'retired' (she didn't know what that meant).

"How about number eight?"

"Yes, I can take number eight. Miss Samantha, may I reiterate how gloriously perceptive you are! Perhaps in the course of time we shall meet again. In the meantime; grow and continue to satiate that inquisitive mind of yours. Now, turn your attention to the actions on the field behind you. It'll be a lesson, for now."

And with that, the bush trembled one last time before her, before the mysterious, hoarse voice of Dorian ended and, presumably, left the shrub altogether.

On the park, the referee blew his whistle several times. The atmosphere had fallen eerily silent–supporters and players stunned–before someone shouted so loudly it seemed like they wanted Heaven to hear:

"Somebody phone an ambulance, *NOW!*"

7

A home player, moments before, had just taken a free kick. As both sets of supporters held their breath in anticipation, the ball sailed into the opponent's penalty box, but only some saw the potential of the cross: others watched the kicker collapse. He fell on the grass, as if his whole body was subjected to an invisible ostectomy, minus the surgery.

A barrage of players and coaching staff, along with officials, sprinted to the motionless young man, carefully placing him into the recovery position and performing CPR. The referee had no choice but to abandon the game and urge every other player to return to the pavilion dressing rooms. Most of the home team stayed by the side-lines, their concern clear for their friend.

The supporters remained quiet. A few covered their faces with their hands, shocked; tears fell from eyes that could not believe what they were seeing. Several suits from the pavilion entered the situation on the park; they were home officials, and each carried an additional emergency kit.

Sam raced back to find her father. He held her tight when she collided with him on the step.

"What's happened, Dad?"

"Just one of the footballers... He's had an accident. He'll be alright."

Sam noted that some of the players were also crying, looking hopelessly distraught and worriedly pacing the pitch. There was nothing they could do but wait for the ambulance.

Some of the more upset part of the support had decided to leave, such was the scene before them. There was nothing that *they* could do, either, but hope and pray for the player's recovery.

"Dad," Sam asked, "there are so many people on the pitch. Are you sure the man's alright?"

Minutes later, an ambulance sped into the grounds through the open front gates, skidding on the gravel. Bodies from the huddle on the pitch immediately began frantically waving to get the paramedics' attention. The ambulance sped over the concrete until it rested on a grassy verge that dipped onto the field behind the goals.

One of the coaches sprinted to speak to the paramedics as they climbed out of their vehicle, to relay to them the severity of the situation. The ref stood with his linesmen beside the huddle, discussing the procedure of a possible sudden cardiac arrest during a game. The tragedy was new to him as well, and he hoped to keep things under his control.

Two police cars entered the gates shortly after, when the crowd had dwindled to almost nothing.

"We'd better get going too," Sam's dad said to her. He noted how unhappy his daughter looked.

"Dad," Sam started to enquire, "what number did that player have on his shirt?"

Since they couldn't see through the gathering of fretful bodies, or because of the man being flat on his back, her dad thought that he had gotten on the score-sheet after half time. It would have been recorded somewhere. Passing by the whiteboard by the pavilion front door, he noticed that the matchday information had been hastily wiped off.

"I don't know, Sam," he let her know, taking one last look at the wounded players on the field. "Come on, let's go home."

Just then, a little bird landed on the terraces, fluttering and tweeting as it had done an age before.

But Sam never saw it.

THE BOARD

The corner of the gameboard that Lauren was seeking jutted out from the middle of the stack of games at the back of the cupboard. She had visions of the whole game pile tumbling backwards over her, like a rudimentary *Jenga* tower. Her determined fingers felt their way over the other jumble-sale items that her mother had stored in there. She couldn't see entirely into the shadowy depth of the cupboard. She had to squeeze in sidelong between an old chest of drawers and living room unit that were sentried at the doorway.

She touched the first few cardboard boxes at the base of the stack ahead; *Nearly there!* she thought positively, like she had been assigned an important Tolkien-type errand and was role-playing it to the hilt. She grimaced as she leaned in; her fingers began walking up the stack of old games and her ribs chafed unpleasantly against the furniture that she sidled through. Up this close to the stack, she could make out: *Monopoly*; *Buckaroo!*; *Scrabble*; and the war game *Risk*, though she had no idea how *that* had stayed in the house (her parents were anti-military ever since her older brother was killed in Iraq).

That's it! her mind yelled as her fingertips contacted the exposed corner of the board. Tweezing it between finger and thumb, she managed to wriggle the board free, without toppling the games stack. Sidling out from between the furniture–then out of the cupboard completely–Lauren took the board over by window to examine it. She held it up to the light (it was about the size of a dish towel and smaller than she remembered) but didn't know what to expect. It wasn't a fabled Tolkien ring; it wasn't *any* other prized artefact. But it *was* still in good condition: the lettering printed upon the board had remained legible; all four edges and corner points far from fraying. Actually, now that she was holding it aloft, it was missing something…

The planchette!

As she turned to regard the improvised pathway that she had been on moments ago, she noticed that the wooden planchette was right there on the floor – right between the sentry furnishings. Surprised, she bent down to pick it up. The heart-shaped object fit with uncanny precision in her little hand and was lighter than she remembered. She poked her finger through the planchette's circle eye and allowed the object to hang there upon it; there was no unique glass placement in the eye from which the alphanumeric characters could be magnified.

Lauren closed the cupboard door quietly. She slipped the board up inside her jumper–plopped the planchette into the pit of her trouser pocket–and prepared to leave her parents' room.

She thought about something on her way to the door: the gameboard didn't have a box. But then, she never knew it to have ever had one. From a trip one day far too long ago, it must've come home with her that way.

Only the dead came home in a box, not unlike her brother who'd arrived absolute in his.

***

It was a few hours after Lauren had taken the Ouija board from her parents' bedroom cupboard and hidden it in her own room, when she found that she still had the planchette in her pocket. She sat with it on the bench outside at the front door after dinner, twirling it on her finger in one hand while drinking a Coke with the other.

Earlier that day, Lauren's aunt had come over to visit the family; Lauren had recognised that whenever her brother's birthday was near, or when his past discharge date from the army was approaching, her mum changed. She seemed more at ease, despite her newfound state of mind and stance on the country's military. Lauren supposed this behaviour was nothing out of the ordinary for the bereaved parents of soldiers–of a child any age or profession–and that if this was her mum's way of coping with the situation, it was her way alone. Except, she wasn't completely alone: she had her sister, and her husband. And, of course, her one remaining child.

So, while the adults cleaned up inside and drank wine to ease their pain and pass the evening, Lauren remained on the bench, twirling the planchette the way a cowboy might skilfully spin his revolver. It was fun and casual, and if she could describe it, this was her 'wine'– her way to pass the time peacefully. She wondered, at that moment, if her brother had ever done this with his pistol. Gunspinning, it was called, but it was not a habitual army pastime.

141

Aunt Leigh came out of the front door, holding a newly lit cigarette. Lauren quickly dropped her hand that twirled the planchette. She didn't really want her aunt knowing she had found the old board again. She didn't know what would be said in response.

"Your dad still says not in the house!" she said to Lauren, without resentment while gesturing to the cigarette.

She sat down beside her niece, sidling up to her so that the young girl laughed at the humour of it. Her aunt was no comedienne, but she knew just how to make her niece smile.

"What are you doing out here by yourself?" Aunt Leigh asked, taking a quick draw of her cigarette. She wasn't one of those smokers who prolonged the hell out of each stick. Inhale/exhale, then repeat. A smoker's mantra!

"I'm just getting some fresh air."

Aunt Leigh took another draw of her cigarette while regarding the late-evening sky.

"You don't have to be scared or worried about your parents," Aunt Leigh said.

Lauren sat upright. She wanted the woman to note her attentiveness. Gestures like these were examples of how they showed their respect and love and warmth for each other.

"I'm not," Lauren said, truthfully. "Not anymore. I've come to accept that mum gets a bit subdued at these times of the year, with Dean gone. Your being here helps her, I know. And dad... well, he's just *dad*. Locks himself away in his office and... Well, he's *your* brother!"

"But you know they both love you, don't you?" She mingled her words with the cigarette between her lips, and a plume of smoke trailed.

"Of course; yeah, I know that!" Lauren replied, a little self-consciously. She knew that was the truth, undoubtedly; but it still didn't keep her from feeling undeservedly strange about being the only child in her parents' lives now. They hadn't treated her any differently since her brother's passing and she couldn't see that happening ever. It was the unmerited numbness of being emotionally lost that kept her from enjoying those family moments that she had spent almost thirteen years getting used to.

"It's only nine," said Aunt Leigh with a sigh. "It will be dark soon.

Watch out for the *shadow people!*"

Aunt Leigh ruffled Lauren's hair as she stood, before tossing her finished cigarette out onto the grass. Lauren watched as the cigarette fell into the shadows made from the bordering hedges.

Lauren palmed the planchette into her pocket and stood up to return to the house.

***

Aunt Leigh visited her room half an hour later, when Lauren was folding her washing into her drawer. The Ouija board was placed inside one, under a pile of T-shirts.

Aunt Leigh closed the door quietly, and tip-toed over to sit on Lauren's bed.

"They've gone to bed now," she told her niece, before picking up a shirt and helping with the folding.

"Were they bad?"

"You mean drunk? No. They were a bit more relaxed this year. I wouldn't say that the few years that have passed have made living with losing your brother easier, but it's certainly healing them and that does take a while. Don't worry, Lauren, you're still their little girl."

Aunt Leigh held aloft a pink boyband shirt.

"You're weird, and with a taste in men that shames *me!*"

Lauren snatched the pink shirt from her jokingly, and they shared a laughter in that amusing moment.

"Hey, I remember your last boyfriend!" Lauren teased.

Aunt Leigh threw her head in her hands, pretending to wail sombrely.

"My god! He *actually* wanted to marry me just two weeks after going out!"

Lauren bit her bottom lip to imply faux worry.

"Couldn't blame him, though, right? I *am* a fox! Even at forty!"

Aunt Leigh acted more like Lauren's friend whenever her parents weren't around. Lauren sussed that the pretty, older woman had taken the loss of her only nephew just as hard as the rest of the family. Aunt Leigh had been present throughout their lives, unlike the rest of their relatives. Since Dean's death, she had moved closer–emotionally and

143

physically–to the family, befriending Lauren intensely. Now was as good a time as any, since Lauren was in high school and without that older pair of fraternal eyes to look out for her, Aunt Leigh's world-weary, black mascara-ringed ones would do.

Aunt Leigh lay back on the bed. She pretended to be exhausted. She didn't just come over and sit around like most people's aunts did, no; she helped with whatever she could. In-house stuff, of course. She couldn't cut the grass or paint the walls–those were Dean's...

Lauren stopped folding her clothes and lay on the bed parallel to Aunt Leigh. The two of them lay on their backs, staring up at the ceiling, contemplating their world.

"So, how is high school?"

"Lame."

"Tell me about it!" Aunt Leigh turned her head to face Lauren. "I ever tell you how many times your dad got the cane?"

"About the same as the amount of boys you kissed?!"

The woman reached around to grab the girl in her clutches, conveying to her, her feelings at being insulted.

After a few moments' fooling around, they rested on their backs again.

"Did dad make up the spare bed for you?"

"Yeah," said Aunt Leigh. "I don't mind it. It's comfortable enough. Unless... you want the sofa bed and I'll have yours?!"

"I don't think so!" Lauren said, rolling away and off the bed altogether. "Ow!"

"What's wrong? Break a nail?"

Lauren was holding her right thigh, her hand placed over the lump in her trouser pocket.

"You roll over on your keys?"

"No, something else, Aunt Leigh."

The girl was hurt. She walked with a limp back to the bed, and before she sat down, she pulled out the planchette. The two of them stared at it without saying a word, as if it were something ungodly or expensive. Or maybe they were waiting for it to explain itself.

Aunt Leigh took it from her; she studied the heart-shape; the consummate, Gothic carvings on its face; its Cyclopean socket, which she poked a long-nailed finger through.

"Lauren...?"

The young girl, still massaging her bruised leg, looked down at the limb. The area throbbed but it was not as sore as the initial pain she'd felt when she'd rolled over it. It was an excuse to avoid answering her aunt or looking her in the eye.

"Lauren, where did you get this?"

"I found it in my parents' cupboard, okay?"

"But you know not to touch stuff like this. Why were you even in there?"

"I haven't done anything with it, honest! I've been thinking about it for a while, and then I remembered where all the old games were. I figured it had to be with those. When I checked today, there it was."

"Only this? What about the main board?"

Lauren stood up listlessly–like a prisoner ordered to reveal the contraband hidden in her cell–and retrieved the board from the drawer. She handed that over, too.

"You know I don't like you playing with things like this! Lauren, honey, I understand what you may be feeling now it's this time of year again, but *this*... this isn't right. We don't need to–"

"*I* need to," Lauren cut in, wavering on the verge of tears. Her hands were clasped in front of her chest, as if she were holding them up in some form of fatigued prayer; and this time she did look her aunt in the eye.

***

They spoke together in the room for a good hour, but not one of those typical one-on-one discussions where only one pair of ears listens and only one's mouth waxes lyrical about their experiences and how they conform to the situation at hand. Lauren and her aunt's conversation developed more into a heart-to-heart.

Aunt Leigh did much of the listening, which wasn't surprising, allowing Lauren to open up about her battles over missing her brother; the difficult transition she faced (and was still facing) moving to secondary school; and, of course, the ideas she encountered regarding the Ouija board and its implications.

Aunt Leigh never once wavered, even though Lauren could tell her aunt was desperate for another cigarette.

"Shall we talk about this outside in the garden? Don't worry, no one will hear us."

And with that, her aunt led her out of the room and outside the house. Owls in nearby trees were the only living sounds they could hear. Far off were the main and major roads that networked into the city, and even those were running quiet. And a dark, star-less sky made them feel even more isolated.

Aunt Leigh lit up her cigarette and motioned for Lauren to sit on the bench with her. The slats underneath were freezing. Some were loose. The smoke from the cigarette blew away into their unlit surroundings.

"So, can we agree we're going to put that thing away?"

Lauren kicked out her feet. Her thigh still ached.

"Not even once? I mean, it can't be *that* dangerous..."

"Lauren, I won't speak to you like a baby because you're almost a young woman now," Aunt Leigh said, in between puffs. "So, I'll tell you a little story, from *my* childhood. Well, teens. I was still young! One night, *I* used something like that."

Lauren, knowing she wasn't expecting a lecture of any sorts, was surprised by her aunt's admission, though not completely. She knew her aunt harboured a clairvoyant history (Lauren's dad, when drunk, would speak of things he used to find in his sister's room whilst growing up: voodoo dolls, books on psychic phenomena; various pendants and candles).

"I don't know what your dad has told you about me when we were growing up, Lauren, but it's likely all true. Now, if he hasn't mentioned me testing out my black nail polish on him–*that* definitely happened! He got *hell* that day at school, let me tell you!"

Lauren laughed–who wouldn't if they knew their dad was once his sister's unwitting nail lacquer lackey?

"On my sixteenth, my friends decided to throw me a party. They had found this derelict warehouse that had mostly been destroyed by fire a couple of summers before. It was a place where the Goths and ravers could go to get up to all sorts–not at the same time! Believe me, Lauren: prior to that night, I'd never even set eyes on the place. Even beforehand, I never felt anything untoward about it...

"So, anyway, we managed to blag some alcohol from someone in the group who had an older sister who didn't give a fu–oops! Sorry, darling! They got us some bottles of this and that, and off we went.

After a while, we made it to the place; it was so rundown, burnt and open to the elements. It was freezing in there! I thought we'd just have a few drinks, dance to the tunes from the CD player, and make our way home. I think you can guess where this is heading?"

Lauren's interest in her aunt's story intensified; and the moment when her aunt asked indirectly for her answer, she disregarded the owls' hooting; and the intense, dark sky seemed to fall around them, blacking out their peripheral visions of the garden.

"You had a Ouija board?"

Aunt Leigh blew out a massive plume of smoke, before nodding sombrely. She had prolonged her inhalation that time, leading Lauren to believe that she was being sincere about what she was describing, for the last time Aunt Leigh smoked like that was in the weeks after Dean's death.

"Someone else had decided to bring another 'present' to my party. It wasn't even a proper one; it looked like they had made it themselves, such was the workmanship! We used a glass tumbler to slide over the cardboard and reveal the letters–not like that smart-looking piece you have.

"We waited until midnight before we began our séance. A fire had been lit and we all sat by it so we could read the messages that were coming through. The drink was flowing; we were all in good spirits just being there, but after some time, maybe before one, I was getting uneasy. I had told your grandparents I was staying at my friend's house on a sleepover; my friend said the same to her parents, and that's how we managed to stay out so late.

"The later it got, the darker it got–and our fire just wasn't playing fair. We had enough matches and lighters, but on ground littered with bricks, stones, and broken glass, it was hard to find materials to boost our failing flame–and it was getting colder. Then, no word of a lie, Lauren: the fire started burning blue! It didn't waver; didn't dance in the air like those once beautiful orange flames! *And it was my birthday!* This shouldn't have been happening to me!"

Lauren could picture the blue fire: it was stunted, like shards of ice pointing upwards in its stone ring haphazardly built by drunken teenagers. Girl Scouts, they were not.

"That was the point when we should have left! It was a warning! But someone wanted to carry on. They thought they could conjure

147

up Satan or any other hellish creation if they kept on going the way they did. The questions they asked... Lauren, honey, it's important you keep away from these things. They're not safe at all."

Lauren lowered her head, having been ingeniously rebuked over her own need to know of the same. Yes, she had used that word: *need*. But Aunt Leigh cuddled the girl in and just when she thought they were about to call it a night, another cigarette was lit and inhaled deeply. After she had exhaled the first of only a couple of long draws, she said:

"But that wasn't the end of my night."

***

But it was the last cigarette in the packet. Aunt Leigh crushed the box and stuffed it in her pocket, and for the first time that night whilst telling her story, she sat back to relax. The erect posture that she had been honing since being out was gone; now, she was seated in an apparent imperturbable position that belied her age.

"Did anything happen?" Lauren asked, without urging.

"A few bangs and some disembodied shouts and squeals from elsewhere in the building, but that was all–*then*. It was when your dad found me to take me home... in his car, that I had my first and *last* proper experience with the supernatural."

Lauren couldn't quite imagine her dad being the rescuing type.

"He had found out we were there; I wasn't really drunk, and I swear I wasn't high or anything! But he dragged me from that place and all my friends were insisting I stay... Truth is, I never wanted to be away from there so much in my life. Your dad was sent by angels, then, y'know?"

Another puff. She was like a human smoke machine sat there. But she was courteous and blew the smoke away from Lauren.

"Angels?"

"Okay, so maybe not literally–you've seen how grumpy he is in the morning, right? But, that night–that *morning*–he came to me and got me in the car, never saying a word in front of my friends to belittle me or embarrass me. When we drove off, he really floored it! "I'm not going to tell mum and dad," he said to me, "because it's your birthday, Leigh. But I don't want you hanging out here again!""

"Trust me, Lauren, when your dad means business, he means it! I had forgotten all about the noises in the building; the blue flame that was as solid as a rock but still just as hot. Your dad drove like he was being chased by the Devil himself, even though he knew nothing of what we'd been up to. A short time later, on the drive, he asked what we'd been doing with the Ouija board."

Lauren asked, "Did you tell him the truth?"

Aunt Leigh slowly rocked forward. Her last cigarette was gone, flicked away into the shadows.

"I did, but I knew he'd think we were nuts. I suppose we were. But the two of us witnessed something that came next, that's forever changed our lives.

"We argued a bit, mostly about my hobbies and interests, would you believe? I told him, truthfully, that I had no idea the others were going to be playing with that shit–sorry–*stuff*. He didn't believe me! Called us all freaks! Called me some *very* upsetting names! Told me not to hang about with them anymore. What could I say? He was nearly twenty and had caught me red-handed. Had he told our parents; I would have been dead meat!

"Then, your dad later told me that he looked in the rear-view mirror and finds there's a shape sitting back there. A shape. No clothes, shoes, face, anything. I remember him turning that mirror; I thought he was fixing his hair, but he told me that he wanted to see if it was real, without taking his eyes off the road."

There was a pause, and Lauren took the initiative to break it.

"What was back there?"

"Nothing. Because I turned 'round on a whim, to see if there was an extra jacket or something as I was freezing. The back seats were completely empty. However, your dad told me that after I'd turned, in the window of my door, a great, big devil's face was staring at him, grinning, like an image projected onto the glass. Instead of braking, your dad decided to stand on the pedal harder; I was almost flung about the inside of the car! He was really freaked out. He then shouts at me, "Leigh, put your fucking seatbelt *on!*" and to this day, he doesn't know what made him scream at me like that, like an order. I did as I was told, but by then that face had vanished. At this point, I didn't know about the shape or the face; we were doing over sixty on the bypass and I just wanted to get home to bed. Home wasn't far.

"Minutes later, my door's ripped open! Lauren, the speed that we were going, the bend in the road; had I not been instructed–no, *ordered*–by your dad to put my belt on, I would've been thrown from that car and probably killed."

Lauren sat with her mouth open, eyes wide, brows raised onto her forehead. Her aunt's tale unnerved her and made her shiver at the dire consequences–and how and why they might have come about.

"What do you think?"

"It's the truth?"

"Seriously, darling. I'll never forget it, and I'll never forget your daddy for being as bossy as he was that night. Why do you think I never argue with him? He saved me. I owe him my life."

Aunt Leigh reached over and gave the girl a hug. She could feel her little body was cold.

"Come on, we'd better get back inside. Didn't think we'd be out so late!"

"Aunt Leigh," Lauren asked as she was helped to her feet. "There was one time, a few years ago when Dean died, that I *did* see you and my dad arguing. It looked pretty bad. I don't mean to pry, and you don't have to tell me if you don't want to, but what was it about?"

Aunt Leigh knew exactly what argument her niece was referring to. She shuddered upon this remembrance, and very nearly burst into tears, for the memories that returned were hurting again.

"He asked me if I had known... if I *could* have known... that his son was going to die. And how I never seen it before it... it happened. He thought I might have been able to prevent it."

OF SLAG & STONE

1925. Rural Lanarkshire.
The Coal Pits.

Thick, uninspiring clouds greyed the sky. The threat of rain as every minute ticked by was more than palpable; on the ground, where captains of industry had begun laying their foundations at the turn of the Century, the coal pits in the area had never been at their busiest. Across the parish–meagrely wooded with lengthy acres of undrained marsh–men of many ages mined the pitheads from dawn 'til dusk, hacking and hammering away in the thinning, winding seams to free the rock which was viewed as buried treasure. Often, the womenfolk and children accompanied the miners down into the shafts or assisted at the entrances hauling away carts and baskets of the rock. Many hands certainly made for light work.

The sky darkened early–much too prematurely for an auspicious autumn–and an obscuring, white mist spread over the land. A young boy, who had by this time seen the back-ends of twelve hard-worn summers, was standing beside a minecart. A few yards in front of him, a single glowing miner's lamp led its owner out of the pit entrance; it guided the miner through the haze and onto a gritty path that was so well-travelled it could be re-tread on the embedded boot-prints in the dark. It was a figure the boy had come to know as 'Bobbin' John', who had emerged out of the white veil. It was his single headlamp that the boy had seen, fastened to the collier's helmet like a lamp on the front of a locomotive.

"The village doesn't need this," muttered the miner as he dropped his pickaxe into the stationary minecart.

The boy jumped with fright as the short-handled tool resounded in the cart, deposited hurriedly by its agitated owner.

"Doesn't need what, mister?"

The old man observed the boy as if he had been accosted in some insolent fashion.

"*You*–breaker boy! The odd stuff we find down there," he remarked, removing the helmet with his calloused hands. "Nobody should ever know about it. I'll bet you've heard the stories 'round here, haven't you?"

The boy nodded impulsively. Suddenly, his interest in Bobbin' John peaked, and of the unusual curiosities that lay deep within the pits. Stories that were, indeed, abound in the parish and neighbouring regions; lurid tales of devilry such as *Sawney Bean* were centuries old and remained just as scary as they were back then, but that didn't stop travellers' tales about the ghosts they'd spotted on moonlit nights, or items of old that they had found; all often wild and beyond-belief fictions. They encouraged fear in much of the biblical-minded.

"Would those be of the giant's footprints, mister? And of the animal bones and stuff that they keep finding in the seams?"

"Pay them no mind, boy. People know what we do: we are bondsmen, lad, and *this* is the 'Black Country'. There ain't nobody like *that* runnin' 'round anymore."

And on that serious note, the tired miner marched off, unsettled, into the mist, moments before his co-workers ascended to the pit entrance themselves. Straying closer to hear anything of interest out of the workers' conversations, the young boy began fishing for anything in relation to what Bobbin' John had mentioned. Sure, there was a commotion going on amongst the miners, but nothing like the unrest he'd seen at any of their strikes. He heard the name "Bertram" and the words "giant" and "footprints" being mentioned, before the rural wordsmiths were warned by others to clam up.

There was one thing to be said about the man that the boy had once heard somebody else proclaim: Bobbin' John was no sweetie-wife.

***

In Main Street, some of the parish miners were being dropped off by horse and cart. A handful slunk away into nearby public houses with their wages, determined not to spend as much as they did the last time they had visited, but just enough to make them forget about the hard-going events of the day. Something was troubling them.

Jack McEwen, a miner who boasted of employment experience from the late 19th Century, spoke first after his first swig of ale. He sat with a group of other miners, all junior men in the seniority ranks to him.

"The union will need to know that we've come across them again," he said. "It may mean an increase in the men's personal safety allowance."

"It could get dangerous," someone added. "The management won't believe a word of it, though!"

The men passed their apprehension between them in the form of head-shaking gestures and low, verbal indignation. One or two even held their drinks with hands that trembled as they lifted the glasses to their mouths.

"Our wives and children will suffer, Jack," attested Joe Malcolm, "assuming it's genuine, that is."

Jack thought it over.

"It's not like we'd be striking again! We don't want to revisit the soup kitchens, do we?"

"No, Joe," Jack replied, "no, we don't. But, there's only one thing that frightens me–and would probably many of you if you knew what I knew."

"And what's that, Jack?" Joe asked, leaning forward in a faux-interested manner–he clearly didn't believe any of the tales.

But Jack pulled him in even closer, as if what he had to reveal would terrify the rest of their group. A secret reserved for two.

"I was down that pit yesterday, and those footprints weren't there."

Unbeknownst to them, Bobbin' John sat deep in a space in an alcove at the other end of the room, and as luck would have it, within range of hearing all about his co-workers' dilemma. He had no business in the creation of the oversized footprints, that was for sure.

But he certainly didn't wish to fill the boots of an age-old giant long said to be dead.

***

The moon cut a lonesome sight, hanging in the sky above the quiet landscape. The wildlife had gone to bed, as their human counterparts had. Lamps were hung in hovels' alcoves, doorways and windows, anywhere that had the firelight chasing away the shadows. For men like Jack McEwen, this nightly procedure of protecting one's home from unwanted visitors that harboured unearthly designs was critical, especially since he found the mysterious footprints. They, according to his judgement, were too elaborate to have been hoaxed; too pristine to have been made by another miner; for each of the men he knew who could access the pithead were incapable of pulling off a prank like this, in mind or motive. But what else could explain the horde of personal, timeworn items found beside those tracks...

Before he fell asleep, he imagined a giant's ghost, stalking the hills and caverns, a sole spectre that appeared in stories that vice-gripped villages. It was thus, in his imagination–he believed–that he felt the earth shiver underneath him, as if somewhere there *was* a figure of goliath proportion sauntering by, making light foot-work of the rolling hills.

HANNAH DANCING

1

*W*e all start life inside someone else.
If it wasn't for thinking of this amazing end-result of sexual reproductive process, Hannah might have considered given up entirely with her current beau and resigned herself to a childless life; time and again she had been present in friends' lives whilst they added to their own brood, and she had found herself being mute in dark spaces of brightly-lit rooms while her friends celebrated their latest additions with other mums. She became fraught not only over the birth of each new-born, but with every thought of her unborn.

It was on the morning of the third of July that the pregnancy stick revealed up to her the news that she both dreaded and anticipated: she was *finally* pregnant. She had bought the test kit cheaply from a high-street store; hiding it from Steve, for he would deride the purchase like he had done before (telling her it was a waste of time, they were *both* barren). Hopelessness and despair sank in when he preached his infertility sermon to her, but she knew that if they kept trying, they would eventually succeed. No need for modified bedroom positions or to gorge on specific vitamins.

Hannah dropped the stick into the bathroom bin. She didn't care if Steve found it–he probably would. He spent under an hour each evening washing off his mechanic's mess. He would likely look down at some point, see the test strip, and then she would wait for his vacillating response. She'd never been one for keeping secrets. Steve had known that early in the relationship.

Steve came home just after seven, stinking out the house with the garage oils that saturated his overalls. Hannah stood in the kitchen. She had poured for him a pint glass of lager from one of the cans that had lain in the fridge since Christmas.

Steve kissed her cheek welcomingly as he slid by her. He smelled like a used motor engine. Their bodies didn't touch; he didn't want to risk spoiling her clothes with his greasy overalls.

"Why are you being so nice?" he asked, taking the glass. He swallowed half of its refreshing content in one thirsty gulp.

"No reason," she said back. "I just thought you deserved it. You smell like you've had a gruelling day!"

"You're not wrong there! I've been running around like a quarterback since this morning: this guy came in, tells us that his engine light's been on for days; I checked the engine filter, the air filter, I even unscrewed the–"

"I'm having our baby."

She stopped him in his tracks. If he were to turn the page in his mental state to try and make sense of what she had just told him, it might have resulted in his own breakdown of sorts; the kind that pulled the rug out from under you when you had just moments ago learned how to balance life on two feet.

"You're *what*?"

Hannah stood before him, the colour paling in her face and her skin prickly with goose-flesh that sprouted mainly up and down her arms. She held herself, rubbing each arm to soothe the tingling anxiety that had rippled over her. She was cold, but only on the outside.

"Pregnant. I'm pregnant with our baby, Steve."

Steve lay the half-finished glass down on the worktop and looked at her. Shock glazed over his eyes.

"But *we're* both... *You* can't be... Did you do a test *again*?"

His staggered retort was a sign he was having difficulty accepting. It wasn't a car he could fix, not a taillight or wiper he could replace. Hell, he could strip anything of old and have it revving like new by the afternoon! But a *baby*? There wasn't a Haynes manual for them!

"It's in the bathroom bin. It's positive this time, Steve. You're going to be a dad!"

Her eyes began welling up; he could see the shine over them. Knowing this was the best news for her in so long, he took her by the arms and pulled her close in an embrace. Her clothes would be marred by his stained overalls, after all.

"I didn't think we could," he said softly, "but you did it! We're not dealing with blanks!"

She laughed out loud at his indecorous remark.

"It's still too early to tell anyone," Hannah said. Her head pressed against him. She was relieved and elated that he was receptive to the pregnancy news.

"I'll leave it up to you," he said, lifting her head so he could look down into her eyes, "the steps on what to do next, I mean. I've done my bit!"

She laughed again as he held her close, all three entities bonding as one.

Even through his oil-stained vestment he could feel warmth radiating from her.

<u>2</u>

The next few months–that beleaguered pre-natal period–flew by in a scattered programme of checks, tests, and scans. Dealing with the pregnancy was a lot different to carrying out an M.O.T., Steve found. For one thing, there was no permanent, easy-to-do checklist– while most things slotted into place (scheduled appointments and medication) other things didn't fit at all. Things like, *why did Hannah have to be sick so much? Why were there so many restless nights? And why was* he *leaving so much mess around the house?*

Steve accompanied Hannah to most of her early appointments. He developed his own wacky images in his head as each week passed, at how the baby would be progressing inside her womb: from fertilised egg at the start, to a turnip-sized, pre-natal human that it was becoming. The whole situation seemed surreal, yet it was one of life's most natural courses, and to Steve that meant having to work extra hard around the home to ensure they'd be able to bring that little life into the world and deal with it.

Throughout it all, he did feel like he was peering in from the outside; the dedication to Hannah and her pregnancy was first-class, he saw. The hospital and health centre staff and their teams provided a prenatal care second to none. He wished he had that type of proper attention and duty at the garage.

Several months passed quickly for Steve, in a mash of motor and maternity dramas. As Hannah's belly grew plumper, her sickness increased, and her moods went downhill faster than a cartie with no brakes. Living with her had become a bit of a nightmare, Steve would think whilst at work (he wouldn't tell any of his colleagues how he

157

felt), so to evade Hannah's blistering mood attacks he would stay behind at the garage later, offer to fix a few of the gas-guzzlers that lined the front yard on his own time. The boss appreciated the extra free help, while Steve loved just being able to feel like he was doing something right without the nagging.

Hannah was eight months in when their world was turned upside down. She had suffered a heavy bleed whilst in the bath one evening; Steve got the call while on one of his extra shifts and his boss offered to drive him home, and said to take the next day off for all the additional hours he'd been putting in.

Steve raced into the house after being was dropped off; Hannah had managed to climb out of the bathtub and partially re-dress; in the lukewarm bathwater Steve could see ribbons of blood swirling slowly, a gory pigment under the surface. He immediately pulled the plug, happy to see the horror drain away.

They taxied it to the hospital shortly after, where Hannah was guided into a room in the quiet ante-natal ward. The attentive midwifery staff ensured both parents-to-be were valued and informed every step of the way. Hannah was hooked up to a CTG machine to trace her baby's heartbeat. The tracer, after some fiddling, picked up the heartbeat through the attached transducers–to everyone's relief, it was a steady rhythm. It was like the sound of a chugging steam train in the distance.

Soon, they were left alone. The machine continued to whir and produce weird sounds that were emanating from Hannah's firm bump, reproducing them graphically on the CTG paper strip that was edging out of the machine. Peaked lines on the paper signalled to the staff that everything was alright.

"You're going to be fine," Steve reassured her.

Hannah, feeling the pain becoming more unbearable by the minute, said to him, "I know."

She took occasional deep breaths of the gas and air to relieve the soreness that was pulsing through her midsection.

They sat like this for a few hours more, each going through their own levels of agony.

Before Hannah's water broke at four past midnight, Steve was asleep on the large armchair beside Hannah's bed. While he had taken the first ticket to dream-land, she had remained awake, sucking on huge intakes of gas and air during her contractions. She felt giddy, more jovial, and it made her think less of the pain. She watched her beau sleep, that oily smell simmering off his clothes, still.

By 2am, their baby had arrived and without complication. The new-born girl was welcomed into the world by her parents.

"Congratulations!" the midwives praised, as they performed postnatal checks on the baby.

Steve comforted Hannah as she held their child against her skin.

"Well done, Hannah," he said to her, kissing her forehead. "What shall we call her?"

Hannah, still fatigued from the labour, closed her eyes and smiled. Even though they had talked about baby names throughout the pregnancy, they had never settled on one that they both liked. But she didn't get time to answer. Hannah's vitals dropped without much warning; the staff quickly removed the baby, placing her into a waiting incubator to keep warm, while they fought to bring Hannah back to consciousness.

Steve felt helpless. He could only watch as everything that was only moments before calm and perfect, had now turned into his worst fear. Hannah wasn't wakening. Her obs dropped like dominoes. Her smile had been the last bit of life Steve had seen emanating from her.

***

Months had gone by. Their baby was home, safe and sound and healthy, but Hannah hadn't recovered. Eventually, she was interred at the cemetery where her parents lay.

Steve had the baby registered, complete with her mother's maiden name. On the day, the registrar asked him the baby's full name, and he told her, confidently, touchingly:

"Our baby's name is Hannah. And I'd like her to keep her mother's surname: Dancing."

THE CARDIAC SKELETON

Rick's recovery wasn't as arduous as the hospital staff had made out it was going to be; the transplant handbook had been more taxing, conceptually: an out-of-date paperback laden with a literary mantra of a heavy recuperation effort. The overall patient journey was, in all its good intentions, a successful–albeit lengthy–and tedious one, and Rick had already begun treading that path. Today was a day nearer being discharged from the hospital's care–and it sure wasn't being done with baby steps.

"I just want to get home!" Rick told the nurse. She was helping him back onto the bed, ensuring that the wires from his cardiac monitor didn't catch under him again.

"You'll be home soon enough, Rick," said the nurse. She helped lift his legs and swivelled them onto the bed. "Once these toothpicks develop some muscle, I'll even be there to *push* you out myself!"

"Ever the sympathetic, you!" Rick said, abashed. "I'm doing well with the physiotherapy, aren't I?"

The nurse browsed through the information on his chart, appearing uninterested but casual.

"After your previous meltdown...?"

"I *apologised* to them! Besides, I said I could make it–"

"Yes, Rick, but just because you think you *can* doesn't mean you *should*. Now, I'll be back to see you shortly; we've a long path still ahead. You're doing great, though. You're recovering well. Probably the quickest of any of the transplanted patients I've seen."

Rick regarded her with longing eyes: she was a lovely young woman; inspired by humility and ethics typically standing pride of place in the medical system. She wasn't married; perhaps not even engaged, unless she had removed the ring before hand-washing. Sharp, fancy diamonds tend to tear latex gloves.

And skin.

"What?" Rick asked the nurse, suddenly; she in turn appeared just as startled.

"What *what*?"

"Sorry, I thought you said something. Must be the meds. Listen, nurse–sorry, *Sarah*–I think I'll go for a nap now."

"You really don't care much for identity, Rick, do you?"

You have no idea! he thought; and with a smile arching his lips, he lay down, took one look at the ceiling and the lights, and drifted off to sleep with his new coronary auspice.

***

May 4th: not the fan-centred *Star Wars* celebratory day; it was the day of Rick's discharge. For almost four months he had been in the care of the prestigious national hospital; from the assessment of his advanced heart failure to the eventual transplantation of the donor organ. What he thought had been the effects of too much alcohol at New Year had really been tell-tale signs his organ was in serious decline. Immediately blue-lighted to the hospital in the ambulance, it was clear to the doctors that he needed to be on the transplant list.

Now, he was out. He held the remnants of his time in a sports bag in his right hand, whilst his sister led him out the entrance doors to a waiting taxi.

"Come on, Rick," Brenda urged, "let's get you home! You can stay with us for a while until you're back on your feet. Pat won't mind."

She wrapped an arm 'round his waist to guide him to their cab; she was a sturdy, stout woman who could easily manage her brother's weight if he decided to sway. Rick had thinned substantially since being admitted, but it was a necessary weight loss. The two of them reckoned this. At the time of the Festivities, he had been overweight; nothing too obese–not like *Celebrity Fat Camp*. Before, he used to sit on the fence on the weight issue, until it collapsed under the load.

"Are you sure Pat won't mind? The last time we met, he barely said two words to me. Just "Hi". He didn't even say my name. *And* it was New Year!"

Rick crouched getting into the taxi, being mindful of the wound from his operation.

"Be careful!" Brenda scolded him. "Let me help you in!"

"It's okay! I've got it," he snapped, pushing her outstretched arms aside. "I'm not *totally* helpless!"

Brenda, knowing this was going to be the beginning of a *long* journey for her, took one last look at her brother; whether it was a regard of sympathy or indeed, lack of, she closed the door, jokingly saying:

"You know, you're lucky you're older than me!"

Rick got the driver's attention through the screen. The cabbie had been smirking away.

"Sisters!" Rick sighed. "Who needs them, eh?"

"You know what their problem is?" the cabbie piped up, moments before Brenda opened the other door and climbed in.

"What's that?"

"They're *all* women."

***

Brenda ordered a Chinese takeaway that evening, mostly at Rick's insistence, which was funny because he hadn't ever been a fan of food before. *The rice was too stir-fried; the sauces too savoury; the chicken too stringy.*

They finished their plates and Brenda left the two men in the sitting room to "try and get on," whilst she saw to the dishes in the kitchen. Because of his new medication, Rick had to be careful of what he ate, when he ate it, and to be mindful if there was alcohol involved. He knew Brenda's husband would have some spirits somewhere (there were only a few beers in the fridge). Four months without a brew! His throat felt like a dried lakebed.

"So, Pat," Rick started, mainly out of respect for his sister. "The shop still doing well? Brenda says your sale season's really taking off." *Shit! What do I know about furniture stores?!* Rick reprimanded himself.

"We're doing okay, Rick," Pat replied, glancing from the TV to Rick fleetingly. "But it's nothing compared to the success you've had. A new heart, eh? For a while that stuff was only dreamed about!"

"Yeah, it's only been dreamt since the Forties," was Rick's reply. Pat didn't seem to notice the sardonicism.

"Good for you, though. I mean, it's not good that you'd been in there so long, but at least you've come out the other side decent. Shame about the donor."

What a stupid thing to say! Rick thought, insulted by Pat's ignorance on cardiac matters.

"They've given me a second chance, Pat," Rick said. "I gotta do what's right to ensure I see a little bit more of God's green earth. Now, come on, don't be shy: where you hiding your drink?"

***

As the days moved into weeks, Brenda could no longer ignore the incongruous changes she was seeing in her brother. He *was* looking much healthier and that was a good thing; he just didn't seem like *himself* anymore. The biggest indication of this difference was the fact her husband and him were getting on like a house on fire–no, like a towering inferno! The witty, respectable comments and chats she'd heard between them were enough to make her double take on almost every conversation they had together. It simply was not like Rick to have taken to her husband like that–and vice versa. Perhaps his outlook on life had changed more drastically than she had suspected. His hospital visits remained on a weekly basis; his intense medication seemed to make up his daily calorie intake! She read all his medical literature with him to ensure she was helping the very best she could. Their parents were long dead, and they were the only two left of any remaining family.

"I'm just going down to the newsagents," Rick said loudly, zipping up his jacket. He had a scarf under the collar; contracting any infections in his condition was a no-no, and he was doing all he could to keep out all the bugs.

Brenda came out of the bathroom. She was in her tunic, a work uniform for the local school. She was the head dinner lady.

"You've taken all your tablets?"

Rick nodded impassively. "Have you seen my keys?"

"And you're all covered up? Just because it's sunny doesn't mean–"

"My *keys*, Brenda! Do you know where they are? And, yeah, I'm fine, stop worrying about me. You can check the pillbox–the tablets are all gone!"

Brenda wasn't impressed by his attitude.

"Hey, it's your heart, Rick. Just don't forget that someone else had to pass on to give–"

"Bye!"

Rick had found his keys under a cushion on the couch. Before his sister could dole out a further ear bashing, he headed out the door, slamming it behind him. He bounded down the stairwell of the landings–two-three steps at a time–enjoying his newfound sprightliness and energy. Although he was still engaging with the daily grind of self-medicating, he was coming to terms with that somehow, he was beginning to feel like a new person. He found that he'd adopted new ways of doing things around the house: the upright, comfortable posture he now sat in whilst watching TV; his new tolerance to certain foods (particularly Chinese takeaway, which he'd grown especially fond of); and the fact he could now endure his sister's husband, a man whom on occasion many years before, he had beaten up after a night of drinking.

Rick opened the main door and took in the sunlight. He had missed a lot of the natural weather whilst hospitalised. Even rain felt funny when it landed on his skin.

He began walking to the newsagents; it was on a series of slopes, up and down. Before his transplant, Rick suffered poorly doing menial activities like this. Simple walks used to make him feel like his lungs and heart were being squashed in the hands of a giant. He'd start to sweat, lose his bearings; his balance would become unstable, and he'd grow more anxious than at any time he'd ever been.

Now, there was nothing. Not even the slightest pang or irregular heartbeat. More importantly, it was not slowing him down. His pace– his steps–were a lot quicker; bigger, more confident strides accentuated his walk. Had he been wearing a suit that morning, some would think he'd walked straight from Wall Street.

The bell above the doorway chimed as he opened the newsagent door. The owner, Aarav, sat upon his stool by the till, watching out the window the pace of the 16-hr world in which he worked go by.

The men made eye contact as Rick passed by the counter.

"Ah! Good morning, Rick," greeted Aarav. "Your sister tells me you're doing well since your operation. A new ticker, eh?! Lucky you! How do you feel, my friend?"

Rick usually appreciated the early morning banter from the Indian gentleman; he was the man to whom his mother would send a pre-teen Rick for groceries, and if money in the house was tight, Rick remembered seeing the old man (he'd always been old) simply write down the items in a thick jotter without accepting payment. Over time, Rick learned that this was a form of charity, an advance on provisions until payday for certain trustworthy customers. And old Aarav was good to everyone that way, providing they kept their end of the bargain.

"I'm good, thanks," Rick replied, hurriedly.

For some unknown reason, he started feeling hot, agitated.

"What can I do you for today, Rick?"

Blowing out his cheeks, Rick looked up and surveyed the veiled cigarette display. British legislation meant that all tobacco products had to be concealed from view. Funny thing was, Rick had never been a smoker.

"Just a pack of twenty Club Superkings."

He didn't look at the shop owner. It was likely due to how freakishly specific he was about something he had never laid eyes on before. He couldn't remember the last time he had a cigarette. In his teens? Once or twice with marijuana in his late twenties?

Aarav hesitated before climbing off his stool.

"For you, Rick? When did you start smoking? Isn't it against–I don't know–your health?"

Rick grew more agitated. He was annoyed.

"Just twenty Club Superkings, please!"

Aarav–never one to miss a difficult customer–pulled the distinct blue and gold pack of cigarettes from behind a tab on the display. Rick was after all, a legal and loyal customer.

"Okay, Rick. Seven pounds, sixty-five pence, please."

Rick rummaged through his pockets for his wallet. It wasn't in the left nor the right; not in any of his jeans' pockets, either. He dipped his hand inside his jacket and found the wallet in there.

When he opened it, he pulled out a ten-pound note... and dropped the wallet and money to the floor in shock. The face on his driving licence, staring up at him through the ID window, was *not his*. When he collected his items off the ground, slowly, he re-opened the wallet to find it *was* his face in the window.

"Are you okay, Rick?"

Rick wiped the sweat away that had beaded above his brow.

"Yeah, I'm just a bit... Here."

Rick handed him the money and took the cigarettes. He moved to hurry away.

"Rick!? Your change, my friend!"

"Put it in the charity box!" Rick shouted back and rushed out the door. Above, the bell chimed and from out of nowhere, he heard in his head:

Keep it for yourself, Hadji.

***

I've never been racist! Rick thought.

He had opened the pack of cigarettes outside the shop but never smoked any. He didn't see their appeal, but something inside was nagging at him to smoke every one of them.

Disgusted with himself (at the way he was in the shop), he had crumpled the pack up and binned them. The morning air helped cool his exterior, but his insides–his chest, his stomach–felt like someone had lit a fire in there and were fanning the flames something wild.

He was at a loss at what to do with his time. Brenda would likely be on her way to work; he was alone.

He decided to walk further down the street, passing the local bakery and café shops, thinking the exercise and the good weather would clear his mind. He had more money, but after the shop incident he didn't fancy opening his wallet again. Who was that guy on *his* licence? It looked nothing like him. The darker hair, the fine goatee; and those eyes...

You know me.

And that voice! He remembered hearing it back in late April, in hospital; it wasn't recognisable now due to the tone or pitch; it was unquestionably *internal*, but a different vocal sound entirely. It was like...

...there was someone else *inside of him*.

He supposed, technically–*surgically*–there was. But stories of paranormalities, where a transplantee somehow 'inherited' their donor's traits (made proof by exhibiting newfound talents or tastes), were just that: stories. It wasn't something Rick had read much about, but the 'science' behind the phenomena was intriguing. Was he really experiencing this phenomenon? The change in his taste with food;

the voice in his head–

From your heart.

–and, of course, the picture of the unidentified man in his wallet. Had that man been his…

Yes.

Rick shuddered. The sun was out, heating everything in its path, but Rick started freezing on the spot. It began internally and spread through his body, numbing his limbs, mouth and chest cavity. But he didn't feel as if he was in trouble, like he was struggling. It was a… *transient* freeze.

After a few moments, he shook it off, literally (anyone passing by would have assumed he was spasming or withdrawing); he collected his thoughts–and *his* only–and decided to walk on for a further ten or twenty minutes to at least get the blood flowing again.

He approached the main road. Across from it was an Asda store. He figured he'd take a stroll into the supermarket and maybe update his knowledge on the latest film and music trends–and refresh himself in the customer toilets.

He came to the traffic lights, just as a young woman pushing a pram and walking with a toddler approached the crossing also. He offered her a smile but wasn't sure if behind her sunglasses she had spotted it. She was preoccupied with her toddler, who was demonstrating some unruly behaviour by her side.

"*Simon!*" she said, sternly, holding the youngster firmly by the hand.

The child, Simon–who looked no bigger than three or four–was kicking out and being irritating. It was seldom a new performance, but the distress that it seemed to cause his guardian was plainly conspicuous. The woman briefly settled the pram on the lowered curb (but away from the pavement edge); its wheels stopped its bulk from moving by resting against the raised studs. She had also forgot to apply the brake–and the button for the lights still hadn't been pressed.

Simon remained glorious in his childish tantrum; the woman had by now, made the boy aware that he was making his *mummy* upset and that he would awaken his baby sister, who would in turn, be upset, too.

Rick was mildly enamoured by the rousing, familial display.

Otherwise, he would have had the presence of mind to press the traffic lights' button to stop the traffic and cross the road.

The baby *was* sound asleep in her pram, safe and secure too; Rick stole a quick look to view the sweet child, wrapped in pink and white, with a cute, peach-coloured bonnet that tied under her chin. So small and innocent; Rick couldn't imagine a little thing like that ever undergoing the surgery he had, but some did.

As the mother semi-wrestled with her child–telling him that the cars that were speeding by would not stop for them if he continued to act this way–Rick felt his arm begin to move toward the handle of the pram, and not the button at all.

What the–?! he thought, unable to comprehend this spontaneous decision.

Push it!

Rick heard the instruction in his head, and as each car whizzed by (with, no doubt, each driver wondering why the lights hadn't changed to red for the waiting pedestrians) he felt the desire to take the pram's handle and give it a little shove. But even though he fought against the dreaded instruction, it was to no avail because now he found his whole left hand around the handlebar–and gripping.

Let it go! he screamed in his head. *The baby, for Christ's sake!*

The supermarket was due its delivery load and as expected, an HGV was making its way 'round the roundabout not far from the traffic lights, where a presumed infanticide was about to take place. And the road on which the colossal truck drove was paved in that very direction.

"Simon, stop it, now! Or we don't go to the shop."

Rick's hand gripped the handlebar of the pram with a strong inflexibility; he shook the bar to attempt to retract the pram's wheels from their braked position in the studs. They became extricated after a fierce pull; but the noise of the pram's frame being disturbed attracted the young mum's attention.

At the same moment, the truck wheeled into view up ahead, its cab creeping in first like a snake's head sensing its prey; its body–a slinking, mechanical form on crushing wheels–following suit. Rick felt a horrible surge within, a terrible mix of callous rage and an incomparable desire to inflict pain and untold harm. In this instance, the baby in the pram. He heard–no, *felt*–that *un*familiar voice sidling up inside of him like mounting puke, urging him to—

Do it, go on! Push it!

Rick was losing power in his arm, as if something else had slid into the limb—like putting your arm in a heavy jacket sleeve—and was controlling it as he watched on helplessly, unable to resist the takeover. A new, unnatural power had been installed and it was *not* invited.

"Hey! What are you—"

He stammered with his words as he fought against the newly-invading source, telling the woman, "I-i-it was about to roll away! I just c-c-caught it in time!"

She grabbed hold of the handlebar in the space beside Rick's hand. She practically wrenched it from his grip, bumping the pram over the studs towards her.

"Thanks. I forgot the brake. Can you press the button please? We need to cross."

Rick reached out to his right and pressed the button. The amber light signalled, and the truck began to slow, although its impelling bulk seemed as if it would never stop in time.

There's still time! Push the fucking thing! Take it from the bitch!

No! Rick yelled inside as he poked the button. *Get out of my head!*

The lights went to red; the young mum quickly pushed the pram across. Little Simon had no choice but to follow, being dragged alongside his mum like a heavy bag with limbs. At least his outbursts had ceased.

Rick didn't move. The driver of the truck, sitting high up in the cab, honked the horn to see if it would get the stationary pedestrian moving, but it didn't. The weird gentleman was rooted to the spot on the pavement.

The lights began flashing amber, and seeing as the man wasn't about to cross, the truck powered on and passed him. Once the full length of the trailer had gone by, even the woman and her children were out of sight.

Again, he was alone.

You almost had it, but I'll get you. You'll see.

***

Rick decided against visiting the store that day. After the frightening episode at the traffic lights, he gave in and managed to find the energy to walk home. He figured he'd be safer there.

When he returned, he headed straight for the bathroom. In there, he filled the sink with cold water and splashed several handfuls over his face. He had hung his jacket up by the front door, so that was one weight naturally lifted. There was another not-so-natural issue he couldn't shake off so easily: the mystery voice.

He could still hear that last threat resounding in his head; a voice unlike his own inner speech, and definitely not one he'd ever heard before.

Looking up into the mirror, staring back at him was not the reflection he'd been accustomed to over four and a half decades; instead, it was the man from his wallet with the dark head of hair and goateed face. There was no way an expression like that wowed the ladies or could turn catwalk judges' heads.

But, this time strangely, Rick didn't freak out. He held the stare with his 'reflection', which did everything he did except appear identical. It smiled when he did; blinked in unison, too. If he lifted an arm, his 'reflection' did the same.

"Who are you?" Rick asked.

Of course, the lips moved too, but there was no reply—not even internally. Rick turned his head each way, maintaining eye contact all the while, to see if it were at all possible to catch 'himself' out; but the reflection was on par, unable to be caught out.

"I'll find out who you are," said Rick. "You're inside of me—you're my donor, I know. As crazy as this whole fucking thing is, thank you for your donation!"

When he said this, he didn't think he was smiling; he wasn't, but the reflected imposter was.

***

As more weeks passed, Rick began noticing the mental and physical modifications of his character, too. He confided in Brenda only a handful of times, mainly to confirm what he suspected: that he was somehow *becoming* someone else. She agreed that the changes were odd, but she didn't subscribe to the idea of it being anything paranormal–she felt a shift in the conventional was a natural step, especially at Rick's age.

"It might never have happened to you at all," she once said.

"My donor," he had told her, "there was something about him. I've never been the best in my life, but this guy was worse. I can *feel* it. I see him sometimes, in the mirror, being *him* being *me*."

She ridiculed him for being stupid; that 'ghosts' didn't haunt people after their living body's organs had been donated. But those changes in Rick were still uncanny.

It was more than simply reformation of his body–of his mind. He even began to *look* different. He'd never been one for facial hair...

It was almost July. The days were hotter and harder to ignore; Rick's medical regime just as charted and going as well as could be hoped. But he wasn't satisfied. There really was no other way to find out who the donor was.

I'll bring him out! Rick thought one evening. *I'll frighten him into revealing himself!*

That night, Brenda and Patrick had gone out to dinner, leaving Rick home alone. Brenda had fussed over him before leaving, making him swear that he'd get an early night and would take his pills at the right time. He acquiesced to both, such as sisters often made their brothers do.

Around 9pm, Rick set his plan in motion.

Closing the bathroom door, he walked toward the mirror wearing only his trousers. The scarring down his torso looked a lot prettier now than in his immediate post-surgery days. Guided by his reflection (and it was *his* reflection), he gently traced his fingers across the blemished skin. He remembered his fear from that turbulent, pre-op time (terrified that he wouldn't make it through) and now, so few months after, here he was experiencing a nightmare of a different kind.

"I'll admit," Rick began, looking into his own mirrored eyes, "I may not know *who* you are, but I know *where* you are..."

No change. His own bewildered expression, though passing in his gaze, was not the response he sought.

"Don't hide from me *now!*" Rick attempted to extract his spectral cardiac cohabitant with vented indignation.

Then, his face slowly morphed in the reflection: his own goatee diminished in its current design, becoming more stylish-looking, as if the hair follicles were *pulling* the hair back into his skin; the head on his hair, too, receded slightly into the scalp, reshuffling into something more modish and fitting.

But it was the difference in the eyes that gained his attention; his 'reflection' had the kind that were reputedly suited to a compulsive itinerant. A gypsy character from those old horror movies came to mind. They were dark brown and soulless, pitted low in the sockets of his upper face. They offered no ocular solace from their depths; no gleam of hope or happiness, either. They were simply... *empty*.

"So, there you are," whispered Rick. He was leaning on the sink so he could hunch down a bit lower and study the changes in more detail.

Yes, Rick. Here I am.

Rick had learned to cope with the unsolicited voice; though it never connected with him during his rest-time, he simply looked at it as if it were his *muse*–albeit an unwanted, evil one. The incident with the baby in the pram was by far the worst; there had been others since–unsavoury thoughts against passers-by, to injure or, on one occasion, *rape*–but now enough was enough. He *had* to put an end to this aberrant, mental invasion.

"*This* can't go on," Rick told the mirror. The reflection's lips didn't move at all. In fact, it could have been that there were two men in that small room–one at either side of the cabinet–conversing over two sinks.

So, what do you propose? I've *given* you *a new lease on life, remember?!*

"Oh, I'm not likely to forget!" Rick hit back, suddenly feeling as if it were *him* on trial. "Who are you? Your name?"

Why? You didn't need to know then, so why now?

"Because I can't take this anymore! I want you *out!*"

Rick pushed away from the sink and began by pacing the bathroom floor and tensing his muscles frustratedly... but the reflection stood in place, watching him, laughing: a supernatural, 2-D portrayal of a prominent 3-D problem.

So, what do you plan on doing about it? Because the way I *see it, you're needing me, pal.*

Then, like something out of a cartoon, Rick could see from the side small plumes of smoke ejecting from the mirror. When he walked 'round to face it head-on, he saw what he had been fearing; that the imposter, the reflection–*his* organ donor–had emancipated from Rick; he had even lit a cigarette in his environment in there. More than that, he was fully dressed: black jeans, boots, leather jacket. He looked like a biker without the bike. That's all that was missing that would have completed this sick scenario.

"*How?!*" Rick struggled to voice; the situation was just too unreal–too nonsensical in every way.

It's just the way it is. You better get used to this, Rick! We're going to be together for a long time–I've seen to that! Hell, you should be thanking me, boy!

"I won't! I'll end this, you'll see!"

Rick ran from the bathroom and into the kitchen. He ripped out the kitchen drawer, spilling cutlery everywhere. He found the biggest knife in the pile and bent to pick it up.

When he returned to the bathroom, nothing had changed.

"I'll cut you out! Do you understand? I'll rip this wide open and get you outta there!"

The man in the reflection finished his cigarette, coolly. He stood confidently, perhaps aware that Rick was simply full of hot gas. As Rick placed the blade against his bare skin, the man moved forward and poked his head out of the mirror as if the glass was solely transparent. He suddenly was a 'real' entity.

"Come on, Rick!" he said, without the need for entering Rick's mind. "We can be pals. Put the knife down! Here, why don't you have a cigarette? *Relax…*"

***

Brenda checked the pillbox in the kitchen. Rick hadn't forgotten to take his medicine. Everything was just the way she left it. Rick had even eaten the microwave meal she'd bought him, too.

When she went to check on her brother in the spare room, she found him lying on the bed. He was sleeping. As he was without a shirt, she lifted the covers over him and said goodnight.

"Brenda!" shouted Pat from the bathroom.

His wife hurried along the hall to meet with him. "What's

wrong?"

Pat urged her to look in the toilet pan. She thought it was a disgusting joke, but peered into it anyway, for Pat seemed genuinely concerned. Stuffed inside the pan, soaking up the water at the bottom and no doubt blocking the entire outlet, were what appeared to be dozens and dozens of cigarette filters.

And in the sink, several blue and gold packets lay opened and emptied and crushed. The mirror was broken, too.

Brenda gasped at the mirror's damage. A crack had split the glass right up the middle. When she looked closer, her face became askew; it split in two, oblique at one side, giving her an unequal reflection.

"Rick...?" she asked Pat, but it was really to no-one. She knew it could only have been her brother who was responsible.

Pat turned to head out the bathroom, but stopped and gestured to the mirror, saying, "Perhaps he didn't like what he saw?"

Printed in Great Britain
by Amazon

35714693R00099